Bimbo in Limbo

C. D. Neill

Grosvenor House
Publishing Limited

This book is published by
Grosvenor House Publishing Ltd
Link House
140 The Broadway, Tolworth, Surrey, KT6 7HT.
www.grosvenorhousepublishing.co.uk

This book is a work of fiction. Any resemblance to
people or events, past or present, is purely coincidental.

A CIP record for this book
is available from the British Library

ISBN 978-1-83975-128-8

This book is dedicated to my friends upstairs,
with gratitude.

Chapter One

Amelia

On Wednesday morning, Amelia Brockenhurst woke up feeling more exhausted than she had before retiring to bed the night before. She wearily opened one eye, wincing at the bright light from her mobile phone's screen as she checked the time. It was 7.20. She estimated she had slept for two hours. Her foot searched the space on the floor beside the bed, and she poked her foot down towards a fluffy slipper only to retract her toes quickly as she realised it was the cat. Swiftly avoiding a scratched ankle, she sat up and mumbled an apology to Adolf the Persian as he stalked off, tail held high with indignation.

Her sleepless night had been mainly due to Storm Ellen ricocheting hail off the roof and against the windowpanes with furious temper. The hail had eased to heavy rain and a squally wind was still blowing hard outside, urging Amelia to get out of bed. She glanced at the desk as she passed towards the bathroom; her tote bag design looked good, considering she had rushed to have it ready for the project review that morning. She rubbed the sleep from her eyes and inspected her face in the bathroom mirror, regretting the pizza she had eaten only hours before; she was convinced the excess calories had gone to her face.

She sighed; she would have to use the contouring make-up this morning. She considered the time. Her review wasn't for another four hours; she would have just enough time to get ready.

*

Amelia's mother, Sarah, was not particularly sophisticated. She washed her hair daily, occasionally dyed it lighter or darker if the fancy took her, but there were phases when she would allow the tints of grey to appear without having the inclination to hide them. She was naturally blonde, with fair skin that seemed to repel any imperfections like freckles or blemishes. Even on her back and shoulders her skin was constantly fair and smooth; an attractive trait she had passed on to her daughter. Sarah was pretty but not beautiful, and she had never given the impression that being considered beautiful was her ambition.

Approaching forty, she had gained some weight during the last few years and the skin on her throat was beginning to sag a little. She was a few years older than her husband, but their union was evidentially a happy one. They had been teenage lovers; together since she had graduated with three A' levels and plans for university. Peter had been 16, having just sat his last GCSE with plans to get employed wherever he could. Their tentative courtship had resulted in marriage in their early twenties, then Amelia had been born one month short of their first anniversary.

They had been married twenty years, and Amelia had never doubted the sincerity of her parents' affection for each other. Peter loved his wife. His manner towards her was respectful and gentle and he appreciated his wife's physical appearance, made evident by the unconscious way he would stroke her back or cup one of her buttocks as he walked beside her.

Amelia took their harmony for granted because she had not known anything different, but she considered their affinity with one another rather boring. There was nothing exciting or romantic about being loved unconditionally by one suitor. To be wanted and desired by many potential partners was her aspiration. That way, there was the opportunity to pick and choose, to move on at the slightest hint of forthcoming disappointment. To be the prize between male competitors was her idea of a thrill.

Amelia wanted to be beautiful and believed she was. But it took effort to look this good. She restricted her daily calorie allowance to one thousand. Her skincare regime was particular and dedicated; exfoliate, cleanse, tone, and moisturise twice a day. This habit had begun on her fourteenth birthday and had continued for the last five years. Make-up was applied daily, regardless of whether she intended to go out or stay indoors all day. Amelia would never compromise on looking her best. It was unthinkable, and an idea shared by her friends. Look the best you can; the value you place on yourself is simply reflected back at you by others; be the best, in order to be treated as the best.

As she exited the bathroom, Amelia paused by the window. The bad weather showed no sign of relenting and looked likely to stay for the day at least. Her mobile phone was flashing, alerting her she had several missed calls from her mother. Amelia listened to a few seconds of the recorded message, which was as predictable as it was annoying. The family were sending their love, their holiday was wonderful, but they missed her and looked forward to telling her about their holiday on their return.

Amelia loved her parents and knew she was loved in return, but often found their adoration a cause of irritation. Her parents were dedicated to her and her brother's welfare, so Amelia's childhood memories were happy ones. She remembered the occasions when she would awake in the night after a nightmare and be comforted by the embrace of her mother, who stroked her hair, reassuring her, 'It's ok, you're safe. I'll never leave you.'

She had often looked back over her shoulder as she had entered the school gates, knowing Mum would be there waving, even after she had turned the corner. The packed lunches had always been wrapped carefully so the cucumber and tomatoes hadn't made the sandwiches soggy. Dad could always be relied upon as a readily available chauffeur, day or night. Her childhood had been secured by the absolute conviction she was loved. She would always be loved, without judgement. It was guaranteed. But as Amelia matured, she saw that her parents' love could be stifling, almost embarrassing.

She appreciated the cakes baked and decorated on her birthdays, but it was not necessary for her mother to expect her to indulge. Mum should know that calorie control was essential; the fact that this had not been considered was inconvenient, if not disrespectful. It was noticed that Amelia was not understood the way she felt she should be.

Her brother Michael was young enough to relish in his parents' adoration. He wasn't the centre of their world, but it didn't matter to him; he enjoyed simply being a part of the family circle. Michael was like the perpetual puppy, always bouncing and enjoying the occasional fuss whilst being given the freedom to explore and advance in his own right. His expectations in life were to see where it took him and to enjoy what he could along the way. He had no masterplan and did not care so much what his friends wanted. He was just happy to plod along and live for the moment.

Michael was only fifteen, so he was immature and did not have to consider what could be, but Amelia remembered the trauma of his early days. She had memories of her parents taking shifts at the hospital whilst he was incubated for the first few months of his existence. Amelia could not remember what had caused her brother to have been so poorly, but she had recollections of her mother weeping, cradling herself as she prayed heartfelt pleadings for her son to be spared. Her mother's grief for her brother's suffering was incomprehensible, considering she had only known her son for a few hours before his condition had become critical. Yet her mother would have exchanged her own life without hesitation if it had made a difference. It had been Amelia's first encounter with the prospect of death; she had seen how fear, tears, and despair were useless. The strongest love was powerless when death threatened to tear loved ones apart.

But Michael had somehow survived, and her memories of his early days had been overtaken by her immature resentment of having to share her parents, her toys, and her time with him. She had grown to love him as her sibling, but he was her brother and therefore was only appreciated from time to time rather than as a constant source of pride or adoration.

Amelia had plans. Her plans did not involve her parents, and certainly had no room for her brother. She was to become a handbag designer. Exclusivity and glamour were her interests, and despite her love for her family, they provided no source of inspiration. In the world of fashion, there was no compromising on aesthetics. Her mother was not glamorous, her father not sophisticated. So, despite their goodwill, they could not help her achieve her ambitions other than to provide the essential financial contribution for her college tuition.

Sarah had worked as a part-time administrator at a theatre since Michael was born. She had flirted with the idea of resuming her studies through the Open University in the evenings, but had figured it was not necessary since she enjoyed her days meeting the occasional celebrity and the social evenings out with her colleagues. Sarah was comfortable with her own nature, and pleased to spend the rest of her time interacting with the family or occupied with motherly or wifely duties.

Peter's salary was satisfactory. His hard work over the years had succeeded in allowing him to climb the rank from a junior project manager to programme consultant. His tenacious character had seen him progress from being an enthusiastic innovator into a leader, but it had taken sacrifice and determined focus, sometimes at the cost of quality time with the children. He had missed nativity plays and school concerts, but had always made an effort to provide support by enabling rehearsals at home or paying for extra music tuition. Peter was firm but fair. His ultimate objective was to provide for his family, but long hours and frequent meetings meant his time was often spent distracted away from his home.

Whilst this used to be annoying to Amelia, her parents' financial support was reliable, so she had developed an attitude of entitlement. She had faith that if she were to share an apartment with her fellow student designers, Dad would support her by paying her rent and expenses.

When she had initially approached the subject, her father had frowned, removed his glasses, and stroked his forefinger across his brow. He had not given a definite answer, but she knew from experience that the finger stroking across the brow was his unconscious method of organising his thoughts, in which case he would undoubtedly see the practical and logical conclusion that Amelia's studies could only prosper whilst living with other creative geniuses. Dad's employment was secure; he could afford to support her, so there was no concern there.

The chances of her parents complying with her requests were good. Especially as, Amelia had reasoned, she had already saved her parents the price of her hotel room by declining to join them on the annual family holiday. Mum had been disappointed that Amelia was not going, but there was only so much sunbathing or sailing you could do in the Caribbean. And anyway, Amelia had been before, so the novelty factor had long worn off. Instead, she had chosen to stay at home, where the house was to be exploited as her own domain for two weeks.

The luxury of late mornings had been heightened without the sound of her mother vacuuming the stairs, as she routinely did before ten in the morning. The guitar in her brother's room had been redundant, and there had been no dispute over who logged onto Netflix first. Instead, the house that was normally chaotic and noisy had provided a luxurious sanctuary during her family's absence.

Amelia paused by the wardrobe for several minutes whilst she contemplated her attire. The driving wind and rain would ruin the peacock blue velvet jumpsuit that she had planned to wear for this latest design presentation. If her father had been there to chauffeur her to the college doorstep, it would not have been such an issue. But without him, the public bus to college was the only alternative, and the nearest stop was not close enough to the building to prevent the velvet from being spoiled. Several substitute presentation outfits were selected and tried. Eventually, Amelia settled for the casual effect: a fleece-lined denim jacket, light blue super- skinny jeans, and her Levi t-shirt. She wanted to give the impression of effortless glamour.

It was not just the college presentation or her outfit that Amelia had prepared for. She had intended to go to the bistro on Ormond Road when the barista called Ollie started his shift. Ollie was gorgeous, a walking dream in skinny jeans, but he was so gorgeous that Amelia knew she would have competition.

Amelia had not intended to stalk the boy, but her curiosity when she had first seen him several weeks ago had led her to searching for his social media accounts. She had found he had a Facebook account, but his postings were irregular, and most had been restricted to private viewing by only his accepted friends. His last entry had been made several months earlier – a photograph of him and a small circle of friends on a surfboarding weekend in Cornwall.

She often returned to his Facebook page just to look at the images, but there was more to Ollie than being good looking. He was active, seemingly well liked, but selective with his company. Several postings had been sent to his home page by girls sending messages, sometimes ending with kissing emojis, but Ollie did not appear to be interested in being seen to be popular. He had 80 members on his friends list, unlike Amelia, who had accepted numerous friend requests from people she hardly knew.

However, she was most intrigued by reading his 'About' page. Ollie had eclectic music tastes, his favourite films were mainly biographical accounts of world explorations or scientific discoveries, and Stephen Hawkins and David Attenborough were listed as his inspirations. Amelia had felt rather disheartened reading this; it suggested that Ollie was a cultivated person, and Amelia had never been described as an intellectual. She had always preferred the more popular trends – fashion, celebrity gossip, and reality television. There was no need for her to study or take an interest in anything historical; the past had gone. The future was whatever would be created as a result of the present.

Amelia's outlook on life was simple, and had been a cause for her to be teased at school; her pretty blonde appearance and her lack of enthusiasm in education meant she was often referred to as 'The Bimbo'. The label was unjust. for Amelia did not present herself as a simpering, giggling bombshell who feigned interest in people's conversations. It was true she was usually unable to contribute ideas or knowledge. but Amelia could listen. And listening with applied concentration was an admirable trait. It was often her memory that would fail to retain information that was beyond her understanding.

She sighed and attempted to think more positively. Maybe Ollie would like her once he got to know her. She didn't have a great sense of humour, because often she didn't understand the punchlines, but she could be fun. Ollie would bring out the best in her; he would make her want to be the best she could be for his sake. Her mind turned to practicalities.

If she could get there when he started his shift, it would mean she would have an hour with Ollie before the new Deliveroo girl turned up to collect the lunch orders she would distribute around town. The Deliveroo girl was too pretty for Ollie not to notice, unless Amelia was there distracting him, which she had had every intention of doing. Problem was, if Storm Ellen had its way, Amelia's hair and make-up would not be looking its best after battling through the wet and windy conditions all the way from the college to the bistro.

Amelia could, though, avoid looking like a wind-battered, average student if she were to get another bus from the college for an unnecessary, time-consuming, circular drive to the stop across the road from the bistro, but that would mean less time alone with Ollie before the Deliveroo beauty arrived. Still, it was the only viable alternative.

*

The tutor had enthused over the natural hues of the chestnut tannins proposed for Amelia's leather tote bag design. The retro flower-closing clasps had needed reviewing, but this was not disheartening for Amelia, and she left the presentation feeling positive and proud. She had received far more praise for her design than her fellow students, which was most encouraging, and justified her trip to the bistro for a celebratory latte with the milk froth handcrafted by the gorgeous Ollie. She hoped he would pattern a heart for her, as he had done before.

Amelia considered whether she would choose a hazelnut latte; it was delicious but would mean she would have to forgo anything with a high number of calories tomorrow. Her thoughts were occupying her as she boarded the bus and willed it to travel faster around the circular road towards the bistro. It had arrived two minutes later than scheduled, so she was feeling highly strung with anticipation. Amelia did not want to be perceived as stressed. A calm persona was dignified. It created the impression of an organised and mature mind, and therefore would be more attractive to the barista she intended to impress.

As the bus slowed towards the stop, she shifted towards the centre aisle, indicating to her fellow passengers her intention to disembark. Obligingly, they allowed her to pass them towards the doors where she then waited, unconsciously tapping her nails against the handrail as she waited for the vehicle's suspension to be lowered to kerb level. It took seconds, but it was enough time for Amelia to glance up and see the Deliveroo girl cycle past on her way to the bistro. The need to get off the bus was the focus of Amelia's immediate thought and she pushed herself onto the pavement, already looking for a gap in the passing traffic where she could quickly cross the road.

Deliveroo girl had parked her bicycle and was now removing her backpack from her shoulders, arching her back as she did so, and showing her athletic form to its advantage right outside the window where Ollie would be serving. Amelia's desperation to distract Ollie from such an attractive sight caused her to rush out towards the pavement opposite.

*

The confusion that followed was a flurry of slow-motioned but chaotic activity. Through a thinly descending mist, Amelia was aware of blurred shapes, lights, and sensations. The atmosphere felt comforting and warm. Enveloping and soothing her like a warmed towel after a bath. Then there was the light – bright, but filtered blue-white and sparkly. Mica-like particles glistening like a ray of sunshine had appeared from a gap in the dark clouds.

Amelia realised she was looking downwards at herself. Yet, despite this peculiar realisation, she did not feel confused or in any way unsettled. Instead, she was dispassionate. She saw herself lying prone on the road, with one shoe off. She looked scattered, her clothes in disarray. Her jeans were stained and torn below the knee. Her jacket had been ripped under one arm, where she had been dragged under the car that partially covered her other arm. The rain was falling onto the side of her face that was visible, causing her make-up to smear black and dirty. Blood was pooling underneath her onto the tarmac.

There were people staring in shock whilst others were bustling around, talking to her and attempting to encourage a response. Others were pulling jackets from their shoulders to offer as cushions for her body. A man had got out of his vehicle and begun diverting traffic away from the collision site. As Amelia watched herself standing over her own body, she noticed she was connected to her physical form by a thin, shiny strand, resembling a spider's web. She felt tingling as the body that was hers suddenly convulsed, then lay very still.

There was no delayed shock reaction. No feeling of perplexity, just acceptance that she could see herself as a prone victim of a road traffic accident. As she stood watching the scene, she became aware of a shadow passing before her, momentarily obscuring the activity. A majestically broad, very tall man stood before her and offered his hand. His face was dark and angular, square-jawed, with dark, deep set eyes and long lashes that created elongated shadows on his cheeks as the light shone downward from above him.

As he grasped the hand she had placed in his, he smiled at her with familiarity whilst gently encouraging her to move forward. As she did so, there was a feeling of weightlessness and she realised that she had passed beyond the scene of herself lying prostrate in the road. She looked back, then had an inexplicable urge to find her missing shoe.

Without even opening his mouth, her companion spoke to her. 'Would you like your shoe?' he communicated.

Amelia nodded and felt her shoe on her foot. She thanked him without speaking, and enjoyed the multiple sensations of energies flowing around her. It was as if there were many currents travelling in their own systems all around her, from every life source. There were streams of colours and sensations coming from the daisy at the side of the road, every raindrop, from the puddles that pooled on the ground, every insect, every blade of grass, and every cloud. Everything had a unique stream of energy surrounding and sliding past one another. Some fast, some much slower, but all were individually identifiable. Thousands of charges passing like a network of colour and sensations. They were hypnotically beautiful, and Amelia wanted to watch them, but instead she allowed the energy that she had unconsciously identified as her own to collect around her, propelling her to follow her guide.

She willingly allowed this man, who she instinctively recognised as her dearest and oldest friend, someone she had always known before time itself, guide her where she knew she wanted to go. Her excitement caused her to smile, radiating joy, as she ventured onward.

Chapter Two

Frank

His legs were causing discomfort again. He wanted to rub the circulation back into them, but from his position on the bed he was unable to push his upper body up enough to allow his arms to move down towards where his limbs would be. Frank grunted. His frustration and despair were so often suppressed that he had almost forgotten how to yell or cry. But she was there again – his nurse, Grace. This plump, dark skinned lady, who had appeared by his bedside one morning and ever since silently offered companionship.

Grace must have sensed his distress, because she placed her warm hand on the bed beside him and very gently patted the mattress in a rhythmic motion until the discomfort passed. After a while, she took back her hand and continued to sit there. Not speaking or offering eye contact, she seemed to understand that by being there, she was a comfort.

Frank used to be confused by Grace. She had an odd way of glancing at him, rather than looking at him directly, and when she spoke she did not allow conversation. It was more as if she talked at him rather than conversing, but Frank knew that she was interacting with him in the only way she knew. He guessed she was shy, but he didn't mind her shyness; he appreciated her, needed her company, and he understood that she was sensitive to his need.

Grace was not like the other nurses. The others ignored him. They wouldn't look at him, although occasionally he was aware that the young Thai girl hummed under her breath when he caught her eye. She always hurried past his bed or looked down at her feet if she had to serve tea to the patient in the bed opposite. Once he tried smiling at her, but it seemed to cause her more distress, so he chose to act invisible because that was how the others made him feel.

Grace was not in her uniform today. She had brought a magazine with her and he tried to shift his body so that he could see what she was reading. She moved the page to make it easier for him. It was an article on how a woman had carried a surrogate baby for her barren daughter. Frank didn't really understand, but he grunted his sympathy when he felt Grace's sadness.

'All I ever wanted was to be a mother, but that blessing was not to be.' She sighed heavily and returned to reading the article.

*

He awoke to find a vase of daffodils next to his bed. The bright colour revived him, but the flowers were removed by a disgruntled orderly who complained to her colleagues that flowers on wards had been banned for good reason. Frank had protested but it had made no difference. The daffodils had been appreciated during their short stay.

Frank did not have any concept of time. He had been in this bed, unable to move, for an indefinite duration. All he was aware of was the passing of light or people. Grace came often. She would sit beside him whilst she wrote personal letters to her friends. Sometimes she would read them aloud, or she would bring a portable radio for him to listen to. Frank liked listening to music but sometimes, especially if his nurse was not there, the radio would create pitches in differing tones, screeching and beeping, which caused him confusion and distress. Other times, some sounds would drift around him and he felt he was floating on soundwaves.

Without Grace by his side, he was frightened. Sometimes the panic would overwhelm him, and he lost concept of his surroundings or his situation. There were times when he would have visions that his body was not whole, and he would scream but no-one would hear him. That was the most frightening. Screaming and no-one to care or offer help. A few times he had fallen into a dark hole. Where he fell, he did not know, but he would wake up confused and unable to understand why he was still in the bed, stuck in the same position. The pain in his legs would intensify and then he would pray.

Frank had a sense that he was praying to something – an instinctive action when he felt in despair. But he could not identify who or what he was praying to, because he had no memory of who he was trying to communicate with. He could not remember much at all; there was no memory of the previous hour or day, just infinite monotony. He could only sense a feeling of utter confusion. He feared he had lost his God.

When Grace sang to him, it was hushed but brought him moments of peace. As she sang, she smiled, her chubby hand bedecked with gold rings on every finger, held against her left breast as she worshipped her God with song.

Leave to thy God to order and provide
In every change He faithful will remain
Be still my soul thy best, thy heavenly friend
Through thorny ways leads to a joyful end.

Maybe he had picked up on her faith, but the hymns united them in a moment and, for a short time at least, brought him happiness.

Chapter Three

Winnie

Winnie smelt the flowers before she saw them. She wondered why David bothered to refresh them so regularly when her failing eyesight meant she could not see them well. She knew what roses looked like; she might be losing her physical strength but her memory was intact. Roses were flowers; they would wither and die within the week. They may have been intended to bring colour or beauty into her prison, but they were simply a reminder that death was not far away. What was the point in replacing them so regularly? She wouldn't be replaced when she left. She waved her hand in dismissal of the offensive reminder and fumbled for the bell that David kept beside her.

There was no need for the bell. At the first movement of her waking, David appeared. 'Mum? I'm here. Do you need anything?'

'Oh David,' Winnie drew out an exaggerated groan, and replied with her usual sarcastic tone. 'Of course you're here. You are always here. Never leave me alone, do you, son? Can't a woman die in peace without having her needy offspring clinging to her last thread, just like he did when he was an insecure schoolboy clinging to her skirts?' Winnie gestured with an exaggerated movement of her hand and pointed to her dry throat. 'I need water.'

Immediately a glass was brought to her lips and David assisted his mother to sit more comfortably. She didn't thank him, although she appreciated the placement of the extra pillow behind her back.

'I didn't ask for more roses.' Winnie referred to the bouquet in a derogatory tone. She heard David suppress a sigh, then sensed him move towards the vase as if to remove them, but instead he surprised her by bringing it closer for her inspection. 'They're lisianthus. Alexander sent them.'

At the mention of Alexander, Winnie's demeanour changed. 'Why didn't you say so earlier?'

She breathed in the delicate perfume and stroked the flower petals as gently as if the flower were the face of her beloved first-born. Alexander, her eldest boy, was the confident one. Never a moment of self-doubt, he'd always had his head held high and his shoulders back. Alexander, if he were here, would not be fussing over her. Instead, he would be directing others, telling others how to care for his mother. He'd treat her like the queen he believed her to be. He'd provide her with private nurses, with her own specialist catering.

But David? No. David, the youngest, the weakest, always had to try. Even when he failed, he would continue to try to prove himself. David could not compete with his brother, he was too much like his father, Charles; always so desperate to be liked, to be loved. David and Charles bowed before others, so eager to lick the boots of their masters, whilst she and Alexander were the strong type, the ones who would stand resolute and never buckle to the will of others.

Winnie sighed with frustration. She wished Alexander were here instead of David. She missed Alexander, but he was too successful writing his screenplays in Hollywood. He was too much in demand to be able to fly home and supervise the care of his mother, so here she was, slowing dying, her body gradually shutting down in the confines of a musty old bedroom instead of in the grand hospice that she knew Alexander would have provided. She deserved better.

Fifty-five years earlier, she could have had any man she chose – the wealthy, the handsome, and the famous. Her beauty had propelled her to being a glamorous socialite, dominating the gossip columns, associating with the cream of society. Indeed, she'd had numerous marriage proposals in her youth, from aristocratic Counts, film stars, composers, all of them desperate to claim her as their own. But Winnie was a free spirit, she did not want to be tamed, to be anyone's possession. So she had refused them all.

Her vanity had been her downfall. Following a suitor's flirtation with another, she had repaid him by attempting to make him jealous. She used Charles, her wealthy Canadian, handsome but dim-witted admirer, purely to make the other man jealous, but finding herself pregnant and risking being made a social outcast she had married Charles. Her mistake in marrying such a weak man resulted in her having a feeble son to care for her in her final days.

The image of Charles smiling with his usual doting expression floated before her. She attempted to wave it away, but the effort exhausted her, so she allowed herself to slip back into the depths of unconsciousness.

*

Winnie awoke to the sound of voices. She recognised the soft tones of David and the nurse Ellie, who was busy changing sheets and organising medication. Winnie partially opened her eyes, but all she could see were blurs. She felt moisture underneath her and moaned her distress.

David's touch was comforting but still she repelled it. She didn't want him here. She only wanted Alexander. She wanted her boy to be here. She attempted to call his name, but her throat closed tight and dry and wouldn't allow her to speak. Her arms felt heavy, the heat inflamed her body, and she whimpered.

Charles was there. She recognised his scent and heard his voice clearly beckoning. 'Come with me, my angel,' he said.

'No. I don't want to go,' Winnie replied. 'I only want my boy.'

Her head fell back on the pillow as she attempted to call for her son.

Chapter Four

Amelia

The mixed aromas of freshly baked pastries, clean laundry, and freshly-cut roses drifted towards Amelia before her grandmother appeared. She glowed, radiant with joy, to welcome Amelia, her arms open for an embrace which her granddaughter eagerly accepted. Their reunion was mutually tender and joyful, until her grandmother stroked Amelia's arms down to her sides.

'My girl.' Celia smiled, holding Amelia under the chin with her forefinger, just as she had when Amelia was a young child.

The fragrance and warmth of childhood visits to her grandparents' home engulfed Amelia as she recognised the smell of a warm stove, the hints of cinnamon and Christmas orange. The odour of liquorice and freshly baked bread encapsulated every experience she had shared with her grandmother. Every memory was vivid and colourful, and constantly taking shape in her consciousness.

Despite the kaleidoscope of memory, there was no confusion or disorder. Amelia was sharing her earlier childhood memories as images, tastes, and sensations. She felt the prickling of grass against her legs from when she had walked with Celia across the meadows. There was a memory of warm breath against her forehead from when she had been held by her grandmother for the first time as a new-born.

The reunion was private, but Amelia was aware of other energies moving around them as they met.

'Is Granddad here?'

'He is nearby, but I wanted to see you first, Amelia.'

As Celia spoke, Amelia was suddenly over-whelmed by the sensation of intense tingling all over her body; there was a sense of heat and then icy coldness. It was unpleasant and the first time Amelia had felt discomfort and confusion since she had woken from her accident.

Celia paused and waited whilst the sensations passed, as if she too could feel the discomfort.

Amelia was bewildered. She gripped her grand-mother's hand for reassurance, and Celia responded calmly.

'Your body is experiencing trauma, Amelia. You will feel it occasionally; it's nothing to be scared of. There is no need to tolerate the pain. You can leave that behind whilst you are here, but you will feel a connection with your physical form for a while.'

Amelia's confusion was understandable. 'Am I dead?'

Celia didn't reply. Instead, she encouraged Amelia to walk forward, still not answering when Amelia repeated her question.

A heavy wooden door was before them. It was wide, with intricate carvings depicting many people, various animals, and scenes of nature. The door opened as they approached and, side-by-side, Amelia and Celia entered a long, narrow, marble room. There were chairs on either side of the room, stretching beyond them. At the far end was a plain door.

Amelia looked around and noticed other people seated. Some were accompanied by their loved ones who, like Celia, had welcomed them. These guides were identifiable by their calmness and inner radiance that seemed to glow within. Others were alone. The demeanour was that of a waiting room. Celia nodded as if she had heard Amelia's consideration.

'Yes, they are waiting. This is where some are given the opportunity to review their lives before they go on.'

Amelia looked at the people seated on their own. 'Have they died?'

Celia smiled gently as she took Amelia's hand and took her to a seat.

'Some are here because their lives have ended. Some, like you...' Celia looked at Amelia cautiously before proceeding, 'are waiting to make a decision whether to go back to their lives.'

They were distracted for a moment as the door at the end opened. A burst of light came into the room; the streams of energy circling the room became more animated as they were drawn towards the open door. The sound of laughter and joyful reunions were heard before the door closed and silence resumed.

Amelia repeated her questioning. 'So, I'm not dead?'

Celia's response was one of humour. She ruffled her granddaughter's hair. 'You are here before your time. You can stay or, for as long as your body continues to function, you can return to it and resume your life. But you should be aware that your life may change, depending on how your body recovers."

Amelia nodded with understanding. She was not distressed by her grandmother's words. She was content just to listen, to enjoy Celia's company. The tingling swept over her again and she allowed it to pass before continuing the conversation.

She gestured to the other people in the room, her attention drawn to a young man seated alone on the chair at the opposite end of the room. He showed no interest in his surroundings. His head was bowed down, his hands placed under his thighs. His body language was comfortable, yet he did not have an air of happiness like others in the room.

Celia followed Amelia's gaze.

'He is not ready to go on. He is unsure about the decision he made, but he cannot go back to his' physical form because he destroyed it to be here sooner.'

Amelia looked at her grandmother for clarity. 'Is he dead?'

Celia nodded slowly. 'His body died, but he was not ready to leave completely. He regrets leaving too soon. He will need guidance, but first he needs to accept it. He prefers to be left alone for the time being.'

Amelia resisted the urge to approach him, but her eyes remained on the young man. 'Will he get help?'

'Of course. He is not alone. He is simply choosing not to acknowledge those waiting to guide him.'

With her grandmother's words, Amelia recognised that there were several energies around the man, offering calmness and strength without approaching too closely.

'He has been here a while, but eventually he will be guided to the other room, and slowly he will begin to review his life and be helped back.'

'Helped back?' Amelia questioned her grandmother directly. 'But his body died, how can he go back? Why can't he stay?'

Celia chuckled. 'So many questions! But it is ok, Amelia, you were always curious, and it is not a bad thing to be so interested. That young man was a sad boy growing up. He felt misunderstood and lonely throughout his life, and he became so lost in his isolation that he felt ending his life was the only solution. When he reviews his life, he will be shown the life plan he chose before he was born, the lessons he had chosen for himself, and why his life felt so lonely. He will see that he had help all along, even if he did not recognise it. With this refreshed knowledge, he will be given the opportunity to try again.'

'Like reincarnation?'

'He will be reborn if he chooses, yes.'

'So, what was his lesson then?'

'His lesson was to discover his inner strength and to inspire others to do the same. By having a life that was plagued with loneliness and lack of understanding from others, he only had himself to support his self-belief. A great sense of survival enabled him from the beginning; his mother was an alcoholic whilst she was pregnant, but he was still born healthy. As a baby, he was loud when he was hungry, the most persistent when he was in need as an infant, but over time, due to having less responsible parents and later, abusive foster parents, he learnt to suppress his needs for fear of disappointment. Everything he needed was provided for, like physical health. He was blessed with inspiring teachers at school, talent as a musician, so there were opportunities for him to use his natural abilities to become more visible and express his needs, thereby inspiring others. Instead, he chose to stay invisible until he isolated himself so much that he felt no-one cared whether he existed or otherwise.'

Amelia listened. She reflected for a moment then her gaze fell on the older woman who was seated closer to the door. The lady's energies were more vibrant than the young man's. Her manner was youthful and excited despite her outward appearance being of an elderly lady.

'What about her?'

'We see a happy soul, eager to share love and positivity with a world broken from war. She was born soon after a war ended, and brought much love and healing to her family and friends. She then became a mother and her only objective was to give love, but she forgot the need to love herself too. A rich and fulfilled life was enjoyed, but she hindered her happiness by putting others before herself and allowing her needs to be forgotten or ignored. She forgot the importance of valuing herself, and by doing so, the opportunity to teach others how to value her love for them was wasted. Her lesson was to understand the importance of her own needs; the more she could have loved herself, the more love she would have been able to give others. When she suffered as a result of not putting her needs first sometimes, she caused suffering to those who loved her.'

Amelia mused this whilst gazing around the room at those waiting. 'So, what is my lesson? Have I fulfilled it?'

Celia shook her head slowly. 'Not entirely. Not yet. But you have the opportunity to discover it and continue, if you wish.'

'What if I decide not to?'

'You may have other choices.'

As Celia spoke, she leaned forward, her manner more enthused. 'Look at these people around you. All of them have lived a life; some souls are prepared to move on, others not. There is no universal law that has forced them to abide. I've brought you here because I need to show you that your life is limitless. There is no beginning, no end. There is no time. This is difficult for you to understand, but whilst you are here, you will begin to remember. You will see that your life began long before you were born as Amelia. Everything here around you now, it feels familiar to you. You knew Gabriel when he collected you; you knew instinctively that you could trust him, that he loved you, and he was there to guide you when you were in need. Just like he has always been, just like I and many others are and will be.'

The tingling increased. A pulsating and gnawing discomfort set deep within Amelia, and she closed her eyes and asked for the pain to leave. It did so immediately. She opened her eyes and gazed at her grandmother with the reaffirmed knowledge that her passing so early had not been part of the plan she had set for herself.

She had recklessly and thoughtlessly disregarded how precious her life was, but now she was here, she felt comfortable and content. As if reading her thoughts, her grandmother stood up, offered her hand to Amelia, and they left the waiting room behind them.

Chapter Five

Frank

The most extraordinary event happened. Frank found himself standing. How, he did not know, for when he looked down, his body faded into a mist from the hip down. He was not in his bed and he was without pain, but he was aware that he was anchored to a weight that he could not identify. There was a sense of being pulled, being drawn into a room where he saw Grace lying on an operating table surrounded by beeping machines and a flurry of activity, as doctors and nurses attempted to revive her unconscious body. Frank was aware that he was on another level to the activity he was witnessing. He was below them, so that his eyes were level with the gurney supports. It was confusing, more so because he was not standing on solid ground, although he could not be sure he was even standing at all. He was floating.

Frank felt a humming vibration behind him. In the corner of his eye, he was aware that there were animated shapes uttering indistinguishable murmurings. They were not threatening, but Frank did not want to acknowledge their presence. Instead, he focused on Grace. Around her there was a bluish mist that rose from her chest and dissolved into the atmosphere above her. He sensed there was something happening above her, but he could not see, and he sensed he was not meant to. He watched the activity of doctors and medical staff bustling around, the lights on the machines blinking. Their urgency was constant, but the scene became increasingly unhurried as if he were watching a film in slow motion.

The mist above Grace had now expanded until it filled the room. Frank continued to watch; he did not want to leave Grace. Then she appeared beside him, her energy circled around him, and he felt warm and electrified. She looked directly at him, then at her body on the table. 'Am I dead?' she asked.

'I don't know,' Frank answered.

'Are you dead?'

'No, I don't think so,' Frank answered.

'You're lost,' she said.

Then she looked at her body and back at him.

'I've got to go back,' she said. 'I'm not ready.'

She moved towards the table, then stopped and turned back. 'You need to sit in the chair. Don't stay in the bed,' she said.

Frank watched as she returned to her body on the table and resumed her life.

Chapter Six

Amelia

The songs of skylarks welcomed Amelia and Celia as they stood in a golden field under a bright sky, a huge oak tree towering above them. The strength and majesty of the tree was undeniable. It inspired Amelia to venture closer and place her hand on the tree. It was an instinctive action, one that she felt compelled to do, and as she did so, she felt charges leave her and merge with the tree. Their life forces intertwined and coursed up and around them, back down the roots, visible as colourful streams underfoot. The colours were extraordinary, and extended beyond any hues she could identify.

Amelia laughed, delighting in the sensation, and the streams of light flickered and became more vibrant, more animated. As she revelled in the wonder of the moment, the tree responded in kind. There was a deeper force connecting them as equal entities. Amelia had empathy for the tree she was in contact with. She saw its nature, its soul, in the same way that she knew the tree was as revived by her positivity as she was with its. Her joyous rapture brought more colour, and Celia joined in

– the three of them creating a dynamic rainbow of energies. But the excitement proved exhausting for Amelia, and as soon as she removed her hand from the trunk of the tree, the energies calmed and allowed her to sit whilst she recovered.

Celia was sympathetic. There was no need to explain that Amelia was fatigued from being tied to her physical body which was evidently still suffering. It would be easier to detach herself from her form and leave it, but there was an instinct not to. Not yet. So, Amelia slumped under the tree, allowing it to calm her and ease her discomfort. Celia waited patiently, neither of them speaking.

There was movement further ahead. Amelia sensed it before she saw the horse that waited for her at the other end of the field. It bowed its head and snorted in greeting as Amelia raised her gaze. The recognition was immediate and wonderful. As Amelia steadied herself to her feet, the horse trotted towards her, its ears and tail upright. Amelia greeted her childhood friend with genuine delight. She had never known the name of the horse that she used to greet on her way to school every morning, but she had grown to love the friend who would approach its gate waiting for her, had enjoyed giving the affectionate pat on its neck and the occasional apple core. Its absence one morning and subsequent empty field had caused her sadness on her school commute from that day on.

Amelia had developed an initial unease and then fear of horses, always nervous of their size and strength; she had not approached a horse since. But now, her memory of immense appreciation and deep love of this horse overwhelmed her. As her arms wrapped around its neck, she revelled in the feel and smell of its breath against her shoulder. She stroked its coat, allowing the joy to seep through her skin as she caressed her old friend.

Celia waited at a distance until the horse snorted and raised its head, blew into Amelia's nostrils and trotted away with its tail swinging freely, leaving Amelia in no doubt that the meeting had been mutually joyful. Celia rested her hand on Amelia's shoulder as they watched the horse disappear.

Up until that moment Amelia's senses had been comforted by the aroma of fresh spring earth. She had felt the cool breeze against her skin as if it were a constant loving caress, but suddenly now her body became overwhelmed by a tsunami of sensations. The sweet, sickly aroma of iodoform engulfed her; she felt her chest rising forcefully and looked down at herself, conscious of her heartbeat, slow but steady. Intermittent whooshes of air were pumped into her nostrils and down her throat, directly into her lungs.

Amelia raised her hand to her throat, which was sore and blocked by an unidentified object. She couldn't move, her body was pinned down. She panicked, looking for her grandmother, but instead she found herself in a hospital room, confined within pale green painted walls, ventilator tubes attached to her body. She struggled, her mind repelling the scene in which she found herself.

'You are safe, do not fear.' The voice was not her grandmother's, but it was familiar. Firm but loving. It encouraged Amelia to look further, and she saw a light in the corner of the room above her. Instinctively, she found herself venturing towards it, now looking down at the body that was hers in the hospital bed below. She saw a bright but hazy cloud of light hovering beside her left hand, which was resting on the bed, but only after several moments was she able to identify the source of the radiance. It was her brother Michael. His head was bowed, his hand upon hers, and as she watched, she saw colours descend from his head towards his heart. The colour brightened into a rich blue brilliance, forming a ball of energy that increased in size and energy, slowly changing into pinks and purples, then splitting into tendrils of energy which coursed down his arm into his hand that was placed on his sister's.

Amelia's awareness was now so focused that she felt as well as saw the energy radiated by Michael seep into her consciousness. The charges were healing, beautiful, and calming. She saw the energy travel around and inside her physical form. All the while, Michael was centred within the energy field he was creating, his healing drawing her electro vital form closer so that the mist cleared until she was in the centre beside him. The air sparkled and vibrated, and she felt the power emitted by the love her brother had for her. She was now so close to Michael she heard his whispers as his hand cupped around her own.

'Thank you for Amelia being here. Thank you for the life she is living. May her soul be happy, may she be without fear.' His words continued as a mumbled mantra, his head bent in prayer, the words repeated over and over. And Amelia realised that despite Michael's love for her, he was not willing her to stay, but was enabling her spiritual progression in an act of purest love. The urge to acknowledge her brother overtook her.

She tried to speak, to touch him, but the words became caught in her throat. She gagged and panicked. Immediately her spirit was thrust with force back into her body on the bed, but just as forcefully, her body rejected her. It convulsed, repelling her spirit's re-entry. The high pitches of mechanical alarms and sensations of intense pain overwhelmed her. It was too much; Amelia collapsed into a cavern of darkness.

Chapter Seven

Frank

Frank had not chosen to leave Grace, but once she had returned to her physical form, he had been propelled away from her by an invisible force pulling him in the opposite direction. He travelled backwards at first, speedily passing through various hues and streaks of phosphorescent light. Then he drifted weightlessly through peculiar faint glows before the travelling eased to a stop. He could see his surroundings more clearly, and he recognised the hospital corridor he was in.

Empty chairs were lined against the wall, but as he went to touch one, the object shimmered as a mass of moving particles, and his hand penetrated into the vibratory glow. The second he noticed a door several feet away, he found himself in front of it, then passing through it as he entered a room. A single bed was occupied by the small body of a sleeping child. The hospital bed was surrounded by childish drawings, soft toys, and greeting cards wishing the child to be well. The child was young, no more than six years of age, their aura extended on all sides around him; a kaleidoscope of blended tints and hues that shimmered and pulsated.

Impulsively, Frank ventured towards the child and watched as the young boy slept. He felt an emotion he did not recognise to be his own rise from his chest until it left his own form and merged with the child's, creating a larger cloud of semi-luminous substance. The door opened and more people entered the room. A woman directed herself immediately to the child's side, passing through Frank as if he were no more than an invisible veil. Her energies passed through his own; as they did so, he felt her connection to the child. He empathised with her emotion and knew her hopes for the child's health would be realised.

The doctor entered the room close behind, his aura a golden yellow nimbus. His energy was focused entirely on the young boy before him. Frank withdrew and allowed himself to drift from one room to the other. He watched as people carried on with their lives, oblivious to the energies that surrounded them.

Gazing around him with a new-found wonder, Frank realised he had been freed from the condition that had, until Grace's near passing, bound him in his immobile state. He could see beyond the veil of a material plane that he had been imprisoned within. Frank now saw with enlightened vision and a recovered intelligence.

Wandering around the hospital in his awakened state, he saw people as architectural marvels;

unfathomable forces centring on living spirits; formations of minute systems of organic cells composing physical forms with flesh, bone, blood, and hair. He felt the electromagnetic framework of every being that he passed, and was sensitive to the charges of energy that travelled from their spinal cords and brains.

Frank moved from one room to another, seeing people in their various states of suffering and recoveries. He saw the fragility of the physical form that was held together by a mental being. The mental being was separate from the brain, but he identified how reflective neurons in one person's brain relayed copies of the information sent through another person's central nervous system cells. This he understood to be the origins of empathy, but he also saw how it could be used as a mechanism of telepathy. He witnessed how the power of thought alone influenced people as they interacted with one another on a subconscious level.

A nurse, relieved at the end of her shift, waved to a patient as she left for home. Her anticipation at the thought of resting was sent as positive, energising thoughts to the patient who watched her.

Frank paused by the Chapel. The vibrations from within intrigued him, and he watched as a woman knelt in prayer. He could see the thought forms as she created them, sending angelic guardians to the bedside of her unwell child.

As Frank drifted around the hospital, he was aware of what appeared to be disintegrating forms. They were surreal, closely resembling physical bodies of people, but he saw them as empty astral shells. They disturbed him, but they were unaware and could not acknowledge him. Their energies were dull and they moved without purpose, other than repeating patterns of residual memories of the material existence they had once been bound to.

Aimlessly navigating from one room to the other, he had no conscious direction other than feeding off the positive energies he saw exchanged from one person to another. The medical staff interacted with their colleagues as flickering scenes of colours and flighty sensations. Occasionally, he saw darker clouds of repressed energies, which tired him. Often he was aware of the speedy flight of souls pass him by.

Eventually, he paused beside an empty chair and remembered Grace's words. *Sit in the chair*, she had said. So he thought about the chair that he had lain beside, and then he was there, seated in the chair back on his ward.

Chapter Eight

Winnie

Winnie had been awakened by the sun streaming in the same window beside her bed most mornings for the last fifty years of her life. Most of those days had begun without variation; from the moment she first opened her eyes, she had studied the wallpaper Charles had found in Harrods of London – a flower design which echoed the style of the Dutch Masters.

The wallpaper was so lustrously detailed that when she awoke and looked above their bed, she found herself lying amongst large tulips, iris, and peonies, with hummingbirds hovering above. Charles had chosen the design because he had always been partial to the Victorian English-styled country home, but for her, the awakening amongst flowers gave her an escape. She had lain in a garden, imagining she was free and without cares or responsibilities.

The fantasy was always momentary, so after minutes of silent deliberation, she would turn and pat the other side of the bed to awaken Charles. His routine would then begin: he would stretch his arms, turn to kiss the back of her head, most likely admire the sun's rays and remark how it was a beautiful start to an inevitably wonderful day ahead; then he would rummage at the side of the bed for his slippers, emit a long drawn-out sigh as he placed his feet in his moccasins, retrieved his dressing gown from the end of the bed, and go downstairs for his newspaper and kettle. Every morning had been the same, day after day.

David had been born, nursed in the same room, then Alexander. But the wallpaper had faded; it had lost the detail. The hummingbirds had long since faded into the distance, and then Charles too had faded away.

Despite her hardened demeanour, her heart had broken when Charles died. For a long while, she existed in a state of shock. His passing had been so sudden. At 62 years of age, he had seemed in good health; she had insisted on it. Having been an active squash player and golfer, Charles had been fit and active until his heart had given up. Widowed at aged 58, Winnie felt she was too young to be left alone, but too old to attract another suitor. Her sons were mature men wanting to live their own lives, and she was left alone to function. But without Charles, she was unmotivated. His devotion to Winnie had been constant. He knew she had been irritated by his ways, but he had never shown disappointment in her or judged her behaviour. He had understood her, had recognised the conflict within her.

*

Despite Charles's wealth, he had not processed the traits that one associated with the elite. Winnie preferred the company of high society; she had worked hard to be accepted as one of them, and therefore certain behaviours had to be exhibited. She had learnt to become more cynical, to display distrust, to reassert her own worth. She deliberately acted like one in power over her own destiny; if there was a fault, she could change it.

There were certain characteristics that defined the social elite, the wealthy class, from the common. Hence, she had quite deliberately adopted an attitude of narcissism. Winnie had only ever wanted to be considered 'good enough'. She wanted the luxury and the respect that being wealthy provided. But Charles, despite being rich enough to be included in such society, would not truly be accepted. Maybe it was his natural gaiety. He was a typical Canadian; excessively polite, tactful, and far too agreeable for his own good. He desired harmony, hence he could not cope so well with confrontation, even if that meant apologising when he was not at fault. Charles had a tendency to back down too easily, and such behaviour gave him a reputation of being soft.

When Winnie had become pregnant, she was evicted from society. People who had once introduced her as their 'dear friend' were suddenly too embarrassed to be associated with her. To be the mistress of someone distinguished in society was acceptable, but to have allowed herself to become pregnant whilst unmarried was shameful.

Charles's delight in his new status as a father meant he did not care about becoming a social pariah. He loved Winnie. He had every intention of marrying her, and he simply saw their progression into parenthood as a cause for celebration. He openly regarded their change of circumstances as good fortune, but such a declaration was an admission that he lacked power over his own destiny, and it had humiliated Winnie.

Their married life had been comfortable. Winnie had never wanted for anything; Charles provided well. He was generous and loving and he worked hard at being a good husband and father. Winnie had not been passionately in love with him, but she loved him in other ways. She appreciated him, and she trusted that he would always look after her. When they spent time alone together, they often enjoyed conversing or exploring new places. They were happy to be together, content in each other's company.

When David was born, they were devoted parents, both proud of their son. Despite Winnie's lack of maternal instinct, she nurtured him and encouraged David, but there was always a sense of hidden resentment that Winnie had not been able to fulfil her dreams of staying amongst the elite. It was not David's fault, Winnie knew that, but his conception had brought sacrifice.

David had been a needy child; he craved physical affection and praise, which Charles gave earnestly. When Alexander arrived, Winnie was often left alone with their new baby whilst Charles devoted time to David. It was an act of consideration for his son, whom he did not wish to feel side-lined by the arrival of his brother, but also to Winnie, who was exhausted by David's constant need for reassurance. Ultimately, it cost Winnie. For as David matured, his relationship with his father strengthened as they discovered their similarities. Often, they would indulge in their mutual appreciation of nature by hiking for days at a time whilst Winnie was left alone with Alexander. She had become envious of Charles's attention being so focused on his son, and Alexander had filled the void of her loneliness. Unwittingly, she moulded her younger son to become a replica of herself.

*

Twenty-four years after his demise, Charles re-appears; he tells her it is her time. She feels it is her time. She is tired. But she wants to see her boy first. She needs him to see her.

'I'm not ready,' she tells Charles.

'I'm waiting,' he replies.

*

Charles no longer stays in the corner of the room where he first appeared. Now he walks around with the familiarity he always had. He looks just as handsome and youthful as the day she first met him. His hair is slicked back, his smile beaming.

His favourite cologne hangs in the air, a subtle blend of warm wood and citrus.

Winnie ignores him when she can. She allows herself to drift into dreams where she is with her mother, walking with parasols towards the church of her childhood. But then she is woken by the pain and the feeling of weight on her joints. Her hands are swollen and heavy; she can no longer take a glass to her lips, or even wave away David's fussing.

David is always there. She cannot see him very well, but she knows he sleeps in the chair next to the bed. She feels his hand resting on the mattress when he is not trying to spoon-feed her or offering her ice cubes, by dribbling the moisture between her lips. Her words of irritation gurgle in her throat but she still tries to call for Alexander.

Charles watches. He walks over to the flowers. He appreciates them, gently lifts a petal, and savours its aroma. 'You need to come with me now, my beauty,' he says.

'Not until I see my boy. First bring me my boy.'

She sinks back and allows the darkness to take her into its folds.

*

The panic rises. Winnie cannot swallow the moisture that has accumulated in her throat and chest, but she feels hands on her, holding her upright, massaging her back. She leans sideways into the chest that supports her. The luxurious feel of soft material warms and caresses her face, and she breathes in the aroma of cedar forests and eucalyptus smoke. It's Alexander. Her boy is home. Her boy is here; she recognises the feel of his suit. He always wore his favourite Vicuña suit when he came home to see his mother.

Joy swells her heart and she gasps with delight. She is almost blind, but Winnie forces her eyes wide open as she turns towards the figure of her youngest son. She attempts to grasp his hands, to pull him closer. She hears his tones offering love and comfort and she leans close to him, allowing herself to feel the vibrations of his heart beating. Her beloved boy is home.

'Thank you,' she says to Charles, who watches.

Chapter Nine

Amelia

The exhaustion disables Amelia. She is feeling a weight pulling her downward, but at the same moment drifting between scenes. She is like a helium balloon anchored by an unseen weight, able to sway backwards or upwards but yet unable to progress. She is aware of a silvery thread that is connecting her to the weight. The light that flickers from this thread shows her it is slowly fraying and becoming weaker, and she knows it will soon sever. And with that, the life she has paused will be lost.

There is a desire to leave the thread to detach itself and enable her to move on. The feeling that there is something wondrous beyond tempts her, but yet there is an awareness she must not allow it. The tinkling sound of wind chimes evokes a memory from her early years of having a fever whilst she was holidaying at her grandparents' cottage. She wanted to go home to be with her parents but instead stayed until she had recovered.

As the memory passed, Amelia found she was lying on an olive-green sofa, her head resting on a tapestry cushion. She looked around her and recognised the same holiday cottage. The place was small and cosy; a two-bedroom bungalow on the Cornish coast. The scenery was real and solid, but there was stillness, a feeling of being in a different reality. As she sat up, Amelia saw her grandfather seated in the armchair opposite her; he looked youthful and healthier than she had ever known him. She moved to embrace him, and he held her for a second before moving her backwards onto the sofa.

'You have a life waiting to be fulfilled,' he said.

Amelia did not reply. She knew she wanted to stay now to be embraced and absorbed into this radiant all-empowering energy, but there was too much resistance.

'Why can't I stay here?' She was bewildered, conscious that she had travelled back and forth through unfamiliar realms. It was exhausting her.

Her grandfather smiled as she struggled to understand. 'Amelia, what have you learned?'

Amelia considered. She had learnt that she had enjoyed a fortunate life, but had behaved recklessly with little thought of the fragility of her existence. Now she was dead. She had died and was in Heaven. But whilst she considered this, her grandfather shook his head gently.

'No, Amelia. That is not what you have learnt. I am going to help you to understand some basic truths that you can take back with you. From thereon in, you will remember these lessons and you will apply them to the life you need to continue.

'This is not Heaven, Amelia. You have not died – not entirely. You have been brought here to rest and you can stay here for as long as you need to, but there is a life waiting to be completed. When you have rested, you can choose to return to the physical form you have left behind, or to be reincarnated into another form on a materialistic plane, or exchange with others in other dimensions. It will be your individual decision, but you have a purpose that needs to be fulfilled.'

'How will I identify my purpose?' Amelia questioned.

She was gently lifted from the sofa and taken outside the cottage, where she gazed at a landscape reaching back for miles. It was not the landscape outside the cottage that she remembered as a child. There was no road, no traffic passing at the end of the garden path. Instead, there was undisturbed natural beauty. Amelia could see hills miles away in the distance, but was aware of individual wildflowers that bloomed on their slopes; her vision was precise and perfect. She gazed in wonder at all that surrounded her, noticing details that had appeared so ordinary before. Every intricate form, every hue of colour, every sensation or sight was so perfect and beautiful.

'Some call this the Summerland, but others describe this place as a realm of illusion. What you are experiencing has been shaped by the imagination. The buildings, the trees and sky, everything that you see before you is composed of astral material rendered by the minds of those inhabiting this plane. It is designed to bring a sense of familiarity whilst you access your life, understand what you may have done or not done when the opportunity was given. To receive angelic assistance and to see wider perspectives on life, greater vistas on creation. An understanding on your purpose will also be achieved. But first, you need to see who created your purpose.'

As Amelia stood there, the landscape changed. She was in an enormous marble building. On every wall, there were books of various kinds, some paper, others were stacks of inscriptions on leather, slate or wood. It was a library that was so vast it was immeasurable.

'This is the library of human experience. Every life is recorded by cosmic memory. And from the study and review of these human experiences, you made your plan. You sat in this room with your spiritual elders, and with their guidance you planned your life and chose your purpose.'

Her grandfather took her to a room where there was a large circular table. There were many people seated around, oblivious to the presence of Amelia and her grandfather, all absorbed in their study of what looked like a large ancient map spread before them. The people were all talking in turns, occasionally there were nods or enthusiastic gestures as they approved ideas. Their conference was animated; their collective objective was to create a life that had purpose.

'Every human experience will provide challenges in order to develop understanding. There are opportunities paved, but it is only as each path is walked upon that there will be a choice to follow it or to choose another path. You will not be forced to follow your life plan. You may even forget it, because whilst there are positive experiences awaiting you, there will also be many negative or painful choices to be made – and these can distract you. There are many opportunities for joy and also for pain and heartache. But remember this, you are never without guidance or help. You are never alone to suffer. Neither are you given challenges that your spirit cannot comprehend how to deal with.'

They left the conference behind them and ventured outside to a garden surrounded by trees and plants. The grass was a vivid green, the lushest Amelia had ever seen. The fragrance rose to her nostrils and her heightened senses allowed her to hear as each blade of grass brushed against its neighbour. Her grandfather sat down on a bench as they surveyed the garden before them.

'You had lost your focus, Amelia, and now you are being asked to change. The life you planned was not to be spent living through ego. Much of the time you have spent living has been unnecessarily made complicated. Your life had become muddled, not because what you were doing was wrong, but because you started to look for your individual fulfilment and happiness in the wrong places.'

As he spoke, Amelia saw herself in her bedroom. She was applying makeup, fully engrossed in her task. She could hear Michael practising his guitar in the next room, her father outside setting up a barbeque as he called to his wife to bring out the charcoal. There was laughter from the garden, Michael's strumming from his bedroom. Around her there were sounds of harmony and happiness. But Amelia was oblivious to the environment she was within. Instead, she was disheartened by her reflection, and was removing her makeup before re-applying it – a process that seemed to take an eternity. Amelia remembered her father asking her to join them in the garden but she had refused, intent on perfecting her appearance.

'Around you there is beauty. The world is beautiful; your life is beautiful. You do not need lavishment. Delight in the simplicity.' At her grandfather's words, Amelia saw scenes of her life passing before her like opaque tableaux of herself as a new-born child, a perfect example of physical form. Then she saw animals at play, trees blowing in the breeze, every form of life being shown in its organic, beautiful simplicity.

'Consider that you have everything necessary to live a fulfilled and beautiful life. Everything you need. You have family who offer unconditional love, you have shelter and food. You have spent so much time striving to be the best according to other people's perceptions. In order to look like a model from a magazine, you have deprived your mind and your body of nourishment. You have forced it to function on low energy reserves, which in turn have made your objectives more difficult to achieve.

You have fabricated relationships with people you do not have an interest in, for the sake of appearing popular. Your talents are being wasted, because you fear that by showing your true tastes, you will not be following a trend. You have strived for happiness, yet have deprived yourself of all the opportunities for happiness that have been waiting for you to simply pick up and enjoy.'

Celia entered the garden and sat beside Amelia. She took her granddaughter's hand and kissed the back of it. She remained silent but encouraged Amelia to look at the scene that was unfolding before them.

They were beside a swimming pool. Michael was drifting in the centre on an inflatable swan-shaped float, listening to music in his earphones. Beside the pool were Amelia's parents; her mother had a book in her hand, but was not reading it. Instead, she was glancing at her phone. Amelia knew her mother was looking for messages from her daughter, hoping to include her somehow in the holiday she had planned for the family. The weight of her disappointment could be felt and seen as a darker energy around both parents. Amelia watched dispassionately, but she understood the approval she had been striving for had always been granted by her family.

Scenes of her life continued to flash before her: her childhood holidays; moments of play with her younger brother; learning to make cupcakes with her mother; watching her father erect the garden shed. There were pictures that had little relevance to anyone looking at the images other than Amelia, who recognised that she had been blessed with more than she had needed. She had been granted every conceivable wish that a human being could have desired. She had been nurtured, protected, and loved, and had received such gifts with complacency. As a child she had been affectionate and compassionate. She had wanted to save every injured animal, she had been loving and caring to her friends and her family. But as she matured and became more self-absorbed, she had also become oblivious to others' needs.

As the images of her experiences flashed before her, Amelia found herself alone. She was in a hospital room again, only this time she was not seeing herself. She saw her mother in the process of giving birth. The distress caused by the pain was evident, but her mother's faith set deep within her psyche was seen as an intense vibration that reverberated along her spinal cord and throughout her nervous system as infinite fine needles of light that radiated around the room, energising and empowering not just herself but others attending. This act of self-transcendence was magnificent and empowering to the atmosphere around her.

The vibrations intensified as a constant hum until millions of fragments of light in many colours were dancing and swirling around them. Then Amelia saw Michael. He was a tiny object of human life, yet his aura was tremendous. His life force was intense and vibrant. But her mother's had suddenly weakened. The life force was leaving her, her aura dimming and slowing. As Michael breathed his first breath, his mother breathed her last. But then the exchange happened. Michael's aura grew until it merged with his mother's. It changed colour from a light blue to bright white, until it circled hers and energised it before returning to his own tiny form as a weaker, dimmer energy force.

Amelia understood.

Michael had given his life to his mother, and this sacrifice had been achieved through the purest thought. He had lived his first moments of life fearlessly and selflessly.

Amelia looked at her grandparents seated on the bench beside her. She was humbled by the realisation.

'Michael was given a choice, too. He has been here, but he saw his purpose and he chose to return to project positive energy. He is your brother, but he can also be your guide. He knows where you are now, and with his help you can be guided back. Michael is already aware of the three lessons that are needed to find your purpose: Live simply; love deeply; have faith.'

Chapter Ten

Frank

The realisation when it came was profound. Frank's lower limbs were gone. They must have been gone for some time. He was not whole, and that was the reason for his pain. He had sat in his chair, he had felt the pain in his phantom limbs, and he had gone to stroke the discomfort away. When the shock had passed, he wondered how he had managed to move around the hospital, because that is what he had done. And now, when he thought of travelling to the corridor, he found himself there; when he thought of the child in intensive care, he found himself in the room with them. The missing limbs did not disable him. His fear in accepting he was not physically whole had disabled him. It had paralysed him.

But even with this revelation, Frank was stuck. He had no memory of his life, and it frightened him. He could not remember when or how he had lost his legs; he had no recollection of life from before he found himself in hospital. He did not know who he was.

Grace had encouraged him to the chair. She must have known it would help him somehow.

Grace. He wondered where she was. He needed her.

His body jolted. The astral journey which he had just undertaken was impulsive. He had travelled at the speed of thought. Now he found himself on a moving bus. The spontaneity of the experience was enough to bring a sense of hysteria that overwhelmed him, but the joy of finding himself beyond the walls of the hospital was an awakening. He scanned the passengers on the bus, fully aware that he was invisible to them.

Moving effortlessly along the centre aisle of the bus, he was magnetised to the back seat where Grace was seated. Her head was down and she was dozing, but she shivered as he drew closer to her. He attempted to touch her, but his hand passed through her. She shivered again and drew her coat closer to her body. Frank watched her. He tried to speak but found he did not know how to create sound. He had no recollection of speaking to her before, but he knew she had always understood him. And then he remembered they had communicated perfectly through thought when he had last seen her, when she had left her body.

Frank lingered, not knowing what to do, but all the while staying close to Grace. The bus slowed to a stop and Grace moved. She bent down, retrieved her shopping bags off the floor, and stood up, all the while unaware of Frank being there. Instinctively, he moved to the side so she could pass him. It seemed disrespectful to allow her to pass through him. As she passed, he wanted to touch her, but instead he followed her.

Grace disembarked the bus. She paused as she set her bags on the ground whilst she zipped her coat up to the collar, and looked up at the sky as if wondering where the cold spell had come from. Frank stayed by her side as closely as he could, not wanting her to leave him lost and alone.

A few minutes' walk from the bus stop took Grace to her home – a modest, terraced house just along the main road. A small apple tree stood alone on a small lawn just outside the living room window. It was in the early stages of budding, with bright green shoots appearing on the branches. Frank had an urge to stay and look at it whilst Grace retrieved her door-key and entered the house.

She removed her shoes before padding along the narrow hallway to a galley kitchen at the back of the house. She set her bags of shopping on a small breakfast bar, turned to put the kettle on, and stopped still. For several seconds she did not move, then slowly turned her head to the side and peered from the corner of her eye. Frank knew she had seen him, but still she did not turn her head around.

He waited, unsure what to do, then moved closer whilst she busied herself filling the kettle. Now they were standing side-by-side at the kitchen sink. He willed her to look at him, to acknowledge him. He waited whilst she turned off the tap, then leant her body against the counter-top. Her hand, still bedecked with rings on every finger, moved to clasp the crucifix around her neck as she mumbled the Lord's Prayer.

'You see me.' Frank thought the words, but as he did so, he knew she had heard his thoughts.

Eventually Grace turned, and for the first time looked directly at him.

'Hello,' she said aloud. For the first time since he could remember, Frank felt pure happiness.

Grace had drunk her tea and unpacked her shopping, all the while acknowledging his presence. She spoke about her time in the hospital, talking to him as if he did not know her at all. It was as if she didn't know what to talk about, so she rambled. But Frank listened. His heart felt it was becoming whole again, and he smiled when she smiled. He enjoyed her presence, but felt she was nervous. Her energy was unbalanced; it was evident she was unsure, and he knew she did not want him to stay.

I need your help, he thought. *I am lost.*

Grace took him into the living room. There were photographs displayed on every available space – some in polished silver frames placed on shelves or tables, others in small wooden frames on the walls. All depicted photographs of Grace's circle of friends, standing amongst wedding parties, at children's christenings, socialising with church groups, Grace singing with a choir.

Evidently, she lived alone, but the photographs portrayed Grace as one who shared her life with many. In every image, she beamed with happiness.

She crossed the room to the bookcase next to the fireplace and retrieved a red leatherette Bible. She opened the book and turned the pages rapidly, searching for a passage she evidently knew well. She smiled when she found what she was looking for and read aloud:

Isaiah, 41:10 Fear not, for I am with you; be not dismayed, for I am your God; I will strengthen you, I will help you, I will uphold you with my righteous right hand.'

Grace's words were spoken with conviction.

She had faith that Frank would be guided, and it gave him hope. He believed in Grace. She believed in God's power. He knew she would help him; he just needed to share her faith. He thought about how he had witnessed the power of thought pass unseen between people in the hospital, then he found himself back in the hospital corridor standing outside a door. Above was a stained-glass window where Jesus was depicted in bright colour, cradling a lamb.

'Remember that our Lord is our shepherd, He knows and cares about every one of his sheep, He will not leave you to remain lost or alone. We are of one flock.' Grace's message was clear. No longer would Frank feel invisible.

Chapter Eleven

Winnie

When Charles was alive, fresh bouquets of peonies, roses, and tulips were regularly arranged around the home. After he had died, the flowers had seemed less attractive somehow, and Winnie had cancelled the weekly order from the local florist. Following Winnie's diagnosis, David had moved back home, and displays of fresh flowers were again a regular feature, but their fragrance was lost in the stuffiness of the room. Ellie had opened the window occasionally, but the air remained oppressive.

David had ceased to read to his mother since Alexander's return. It had been Winnie's request. She preferred to hear Alexander's slow and careful drawl, with a hint of the American accent he had acquired during the years he had spent living there, as he spoke about his work or his home. She liked to hear about his opulent lifestyle, to be given descriptions of his expensive cars, to hear the gossip about his celebrity friends. She didn't know any of them, of course, but that didn't matter. The fact that they were rich and famous was all she really cared about.

David did not fuss over her as much. Whilst Alexander was there, he would stay in another room and allow them time together.

Winnie would confide in Alexander about his brother. 'He can be a nuisance, always fussing over me. I prefer you to be here. So stay until I am dead and buried.'

Charles's presence was constant. He waited patiently, ready to take her with him, but she was reluctant to leave Alexander. Now that he was here, she wanted to spend time with him. She would say this often, but sometimes the exhaustion would overwhelm and confuse her, and she would think it was David's, not Alexander's facial contours she was stroking.

*

Charles began to accompany her in her dreams. They would wander around the garden enjoying the scent of freshly cut grass and lavender. Winnie's hand rested on Charles's crooked arm as he pointed out the blooms and marvelled at their individual beauty. His appreciation for nature was always expressed with sincerity. It was little wonder he had inspired David with such a passion for botany. His awe for nature could be infectious, for now Winnie often found herself cheered at the first sound of frogs chirping; she recognised it as the beginning of spring.

The sound of seagulls no longer brought her irritation. Charles had encouraged her to consider them not as vermin but as symbols of freedom. He described a seagull's caw as the sounds associated with carefree summer days, and reminded her of a day they had spent on the beach when the children had built a sandcastle. Winnie had prolonged their play until the tide was almost in, insisting it had to be made more decadent by adding seashells and a cocktail umbrella to their crafted citadel. Charles chuckled. 'You had standards,' he said with a smile.

*

The nurse had administered a larger dose of morphine. Winnie sank into a white fog as the relief swept over her. Distorted images whirled around her mind before Charles appeared.

'Come with me, my girl.' He took her hand and led her into the garden. Fairy lights hung from every tree. Balloons bobbed and swayed in the breeze, and the scent of caramelised sugar wafted towards them.

The melody of the *Parisian Waltz* increased in volume as they approached the carousel. The high-pitched, nasal twangs of a hurdy-gurdy and accompanying bellows of the accordion vibrated around them.

Charles offered his hand as Winnie stepped onto the rotating platform, and guided her towards the nearest horse. 'Do you remember this, my girl?'

As Winnie mounted the horse, the delight within her bubbled forth and caused her to giggle. Yes, she remembered.

In June 1969, Winnie and Charles had been present at a dinner party attended by dignitaries and the popular television celebrities and supermodels of that era. Charles spent time with John Lennon as they discussed the musician's forthcoming visit to Canada, whilst Winnie had been excited by the prospect of meeting Countess of Snowden, Princess Margaret, who was rumoured to have been invited.

With such anticipation in mind, Winnie had behaved in a manner that she considered appropriate. She had perfected an aloof air, holding her *quellazaire* in a manner emulating her royal idol, and dismissing guests she considered to be from lower ranks. She had wandered around the party, confident that she looked sensational in her full-length, navy silk Dior evening gown that accentuated her curves to their advantage, despite her rebelling against the trend of mini-skirts. Her brazen disregard for the current fashion had not been wrong, made evident by the looks of admiration from the men and the envious glares from their female companions.

Charles had progressed from his amiable chatting to downing more whisky as the evening wore on. Winnie had not noticed the antics of her husband until she heard a ruckus coming from the corner of the room. To her dismay, she saw Charles, in a moment of intoxicated mischief, had stretched the skin from his face towards his ears with Sellotape, declaring himself inspired by Hedy Lamarr's recent facelift. The room had buzzed with shock and

drunken hilarity, whilst Winne had been so morti-
fied that she had left the party.

Charles had run out after her, dismissed the cab
she had hailed, and marched her down the road
where there was a funfair. 'If you are so high and
mighty, get back on your high horse!' he had curtly
ordered, directing her onto the carousel in a rare
display of authority. In surprise, Winnie had oblig-
ed. She had not admitted to Charles that the time
spent at the funfair had been the highlight of her
evening.

*

Winnie understood Charles's visitations were intended to give her comfort. The pain medication
could cause nightmares, but the fear eased when he
was there. Charles's love for Winnie had remained
constant in life and death. He had been loyal and
true to her. She saw this now more than ever and it
relieved her anxiety, but she would never say. She
had no wish to punish him for her disappointment
in life, but still she considered Charles had been an
ordinary man, and that had meant she had become
ordinary as well.

It had not been the life she had wanted. She had
not lived in luxury; she lived in comfort. She was
not surrounded by friends in her last days. She was
socially isolated without visitors. There were no
well-wishers. David, Ellie the nurse, and occasionally the doctor were her only companions. If it

were not for Alexander's unexpected appearance at her bedside, she would be dying with a broken heart and mind.

She had awoken with Alexander massaging her swollen hands with rose fragranced hand cream. 'Make this house yours,' she mumbled.

'Bring your wealthy friends to this house, have parties, make this house come alive. David will make this house dull and practical. Don't let him take the house. Make it yours.'

She had made Alexander promise, and he had soothed her with words of reassurance. She had wanted to sign the relevant papers, but would drift off into a dreamless sleep before she was able.

Chapter Twelve

Amelia

Amelia was looking up at an expanse created by shimmering light. She stood within a dome-shaped building, similar to an enormous observatory. The walls looked solid, but as she approached them, she realised they were moving as one phenomenal mass.

Above her there were constant streams of light, like microscopic comets, varying in brightness or strength but all shooting towards one direction, all heading into what appeared to be infinity.

Amelia watched them. She had a sense of what they were: prayers of every living soul.

'No prayer is ever ignored. They are always heard, always noted within the cosmic memory. A prayer is a message from the soul. It raises the highest quality of the mind and enables communication between states of consciousness.'

Celia had entered the building behind Amelia. She placed her hand on her granddaughter's shoulder and they adopted a stance as if they were stargazing.

'I heard your prayer when I passed over, Amelia. I heard your message of love and I felt the healing you were sending me; it helped me. It propelled me. You were a young child, but you understood what love was and you projected it. That is what a prayer is. As you matured, you abandoned all idea of prayers. You saw it as being a religious habit that was old-fashioned and traditional, and the meaning of prayer was nothing more than a reflection of how virtue can be surrendered to un-necessary desires.

'During the course of most human experiences, it is forgotten that what is wanted is not what is needed. There are prayers that mortgage applications will be approved, driving tests will be passed, that employment will be offered. These types of prayers you can see as tiny, duller fragments. They lack strength and, in some cases, they lack meaning, because the soul is conscious that what is being asked is not appropriate for their evolvement. A prayer is more than just a wish. It is not meant to provide a short-cut to being given what is desired.

'When people are afraid, they pray. When people are hopeful, they pray. When they are lonely or sad or in despair, they pray. So, prayer is sometimes a request for help which is unnecessary. Asking for something that they recognise as being missing means they are focusing on what is negative. Still, the prayers are heard, and they are always answered regardless whether the answer is recognised. Help is always given. No life-force is ever left alone without guidance or support. It is not always possible for your guides to intervene, especially if the plan was to confront certain challenges in order to achieve a purpose, but there are many occasions when a life doesn't follow the path that was laid before them and that is when life can feel uncomfortable. That is when many people pray for guidance.

'The larger and more forceful balls of light you see being projected are the prayers that are thankful. Such prayers truly make a difference to all living experience. When one projects true gratitude, they are focusing on positive energy and they are manifesting it back to the universe.'

Amelia was puzzled. 'So, prayer is not to ask God for guidance?'

Celia smiled. 'Of course, it can be. And if the intention is for it to be heard as such, then that is how it will be received.'

'So, there is a God?'

Celia nodded. 'Yes, if you have that understanding. Whatever you believe during your life, you will continue to believe in the next phase, at the end of that life.'

She guided Amelia outside and instructed her to look up at what appeared to be a bright blue sky.

'There are many that believe Heaven is in the sky, Hell is below ground. But imagine that this dimension where you find yourself with me now, is just on one layer of an enormous rainbow. Around us there are many other layers, other dimensions all happening in the same moment. These layers have several sub-planes, and within those, sub-divisions.

There are numerous kinds of matter and forms that extend beyond the realms of the imagination that you can comprehend here. So, within this dimension, which is one of many material planes, we can see and experience life in a similar way as we did before we got here. It is solid and it is real; it is healthier and happier, there is no darkness.

'We are here to reflect on our lives, therefore it is not much different to what we were accustomed to, but as we learn to relinquish our egos, we exist simply. We understand that we have everything we need; we don't need anything other than to exist. Your body is simply an avatar that allows you to explore, but as you advance in your understanding of the different dimensions, your mind returns to a higher frequency. You will abandon the idea of having a physical vehicle, because your mind will contain all realities. It will perceive all other dimensions, the earth pull will lessen, and the soul will elevate to become a highly energised intellect and spirit; an immortal pure thought which has fulfilled all purpose in the evolution of cosmic consciousness. Ultimately, you will discover an advanced spiritual nature, and with it the understanding that all levels are created by the one energy source – the brightest light, or as some may call it, God.'

Amelia considered this. 'So, what is Hell?'

'Hell is not always a punishment level, neither is it a vast pit where there is eternal suffering. But it is a darker place because the light is filtered from the highest energy source through the layered dimensions. So, where there is less light, there is less vision, less understanding. Souls at the lowest level are driven by ego, through desires that they constantly strive to feed, so there is the need to achieve their desires at any cost. They do not care about other souls; they do not experience love in its purest form. They are tormented by the lack of a physical vehicle that allows them to fulfil their desires.'

'So, it is true that those who intentionally cause harm to others go to Hell?'

Celia considered this. She brought up a memory of a news article Amelia had commented on recently. Amelia saw herself reading the news headlines to her friends at college. A student from a neighbouring college had been charged with the planned murder of a classmate following her public rejection of his advances. Amelia heard herself commenting that the perpetrator deserved to have the same death inflicted on him.

'The boy who committed the action was not evil. He had had good thoughts, and he had projected love and healing to many people within communities he had been in contact with throughout his life. If you could see his thoughts and his love for others, you would not see him as a bad person, but you would wish him to have healing for his confusion. Depending on what choices he makes from now, he has every chance of seeing what you are seeing now.'

'So, he won't end up in Hell, even though he willingly took the life of another?'

Celia shook her head. 'No, he has the potential to recognise what and why he did wrong, and counterbalance it by projecting positive energy with pure thought for others. A soul that stays on the lowest level usually has no understanding of love, nor has the ability to share positive energy. They enjoy creating negative energy and seeing how it destroys. Occasionally, they are able to influence a living being as an instrument for their mischief. Those who dull their senses through drugs or alcohol are more susceptible to being used in such a way. But, always, they are guided and helped.'

'So, there are evil souls?'

Celia shook her head again. 'No, there is no evil in any soul. Cruel or damaging behaviours are borne out of ignorance and the absence of love. Ultimately, every soul is sustained by love. But there can be misunderstanding as to what love is. When pleasure is misconstrued as self-love, there becomes a need to satisfy it, because love is sought. Such is their desire to be reborn with a physical body, as they seek to be pleasured or loved, they head towards reincarnation on a low plane. Even the most degraded souls eventually seek their way to higher planes, because they are denied satisfaction any other way.'

Amelia looked around her. Everything was so perfect. Surely she could learn all that she needed to here?

Celia smiled and shook her head. 'No, Amelia. You will not fulfil your purpose here. Already you have learnt that your life will improve once you have learnt to accept yourself utterly. Your body, your experiences, and your understanding of the world around you is for your benefit and for your appreciation only. You can be content with all that you have. You do not need to elaborate your existence in order to be fulfilled. You have also learnt that you chose your life; you planned it! But there is one lesson in particular you need to learn before you progress, and that is to recognise one of the greatest gifts of all.'

Chapter Thirteen

Frank

Frank's astral travels gave him a sense of freedom. He enjoyed being able to travel down a street as if he were physically complete again. Once, he had watched a bird and wondered what it would feel like to fly, but as soon as he had thought it, he found himself flying above the heads of people and buildings. When he looked down, he noticed how each building had its own atmosphere that was created by the collective thoughts of the people frequenting them. Over time, he discovered that the potential to explore further was limitless. He had flown beside a bird, then a plane, and then, as the fancy took him, he found himself travelling the extent of the celestial dome. Below him a multitude of tiny illuminated sparks shone. He recognised a difference between the artificial lights man had created from the fiery particles that represented every living soul.

As he continued his astral exploration, Frank discovered he possessed more power in his mind than he had ever thought possible. He witnessed solar winds interacting with the earth's magnetic field, and saw how it influenced fluids in living bodies, reacting as highly conductive memory bodies for low-frequency electrical waves. With this understanding, he experimented changing the course of a bird's flight by thinking it should go in the opposite direction. Then he would send thoughts to infants in prams, projecting calm as they wailed with hunger.

There was no inclination to manifest negative thoughts or actions in any living body, but Frank could see how it was possible to communicate, if not manipulate, the minds of others. It could become more than simply using telepathy, but Frank had no desire to exploit his newly-discovered skill. Instead, he wondered if it would be a method of communicating directly to Grace. He had seen her aura and recognised that Grace's spiritual faith influenced her to focus on positive thoughts. With the highest quality of her mind, she was automatically more receptive to receiving his messages through her subconscious.

*

Frank did not like being invisible; the loneliness was sufferable. Dogs and cats were particularly sensitive to his presence, so Frank preferred to seek the company of animals. He found after their initial unease, after they had barked or spat in his direction, they would settle and follow his telepathed reassurance that he did not wish them harm. Horses and livestock were particularly gentle with him.

Frank found that they lived their lives in anxiety, never knowing when they would be moved on or taken away from their stable-mates. They were constantly dominated by the wills of their masters, and as such they understood the pain of loss and showed empathy towards all lost souls.

Frank had no direction. He had the freedom to travel where his thoughts took him, yet he was still bound within the confines of his own amnesia. There was a profound sense of loss within him, and a need to find himself, his physical body. He needed to know why he was not like the living, yet surely he was not dead? When these thoughts entered his mind, he would either return to the hospital or he would think of Grace, seeking her comfort. It was difficult to gauge how regularly he visited Grace, because his perception of time was distorted and confusing, but he noticed that the apple tree in her front garden had grown taller since he had first followed her home.

It was evident her health had deteriorated since he had last been there; her vibrations were slower, her responses sluggish. Frank could see that Grace's brush with death had been the result of a failing heart. He stayed by her side. He did not know how to ease her discomfort, but he imagined that by being there he was giving her healing in the same way she had cared for him. Her physical health was compromised, but she was resilient. She dozed frequently, and he would ease her suffering by imagining he was singing to her. He remembered the hymns she had sung to him, and he sang the same to her. Then, on a moment's whim, he audaciously entered her dreams and asked her for help to identify him.

*

Frank did not remember leaving Grace. He awoke back in the hospital, feeling an urge to be with Grace as she held him in her thoughts. The pull was exceptionally strong, and he identified that it was not his own need that magnetised him to her, but that she was calling him. He did not hear it, but felt the strength of her beckoning.

The apple tree was bedecked with blossom flowers. Time had passed; time that Frank had been unaware of.

The energy around Grace was different. It was thinner and vibrating slower than was usual, but the sensation was comforting and inviting to Frank. Grace was not alone. She was seated opposite a woman who appeared very still, as if she were in a dream state. Her eyes were closed, her arms outstretched, as her etheric matter separated from her physical state and accumulated behind.

As the energy manifested around her physical body, empowering her projection, Frank drew closer until his aura merged with hers. He felt the medium's reception of him. She recognised a presence was there and welcomed him to read her energies.

'I sense a male spirit here.' The medium spoke aloud and directed her information to Grace, who nodded but remained quiet.

'I'm not a spirit,' Frank interjected.

The medium understood his confusion, for she could read his uncertainty.

'He is an older man. A man of great courage and good character. He means no harm to you, but he believes you can help him.'

Frank realised the medium was talking about him, telling Grace what she could sense. It was disconcerting, but there was truth in what the medium was relaying. He urged the woman to read him further and came closer to her.

'I see he wore a uniform. He was hurt very badly.' The woman was concentrating. She could feel the warmth of Frank's close presence, and she was thanking him, encouraging him, all the while translating her reading to Grace. 'There is confusion around him,' she said. 'I feel that his heart is burdened because he has unfinished business. He was not ready to leave without saying goodbye to his loved ones.'

Grace had moved forward on the sofa. She sat with her hands cupped together, and Frank could see that she was unconsciously sending her own energies to empower the communion.

The medium was having difficulty; the charges around her were flickering and losing their strength. Inquisitive disembodied spectres were attracted by the vibrations and had trespassed to satisfy their curiosity. Their souls had already departed to a higher plane, but the remaining entities were there to take impressions from the mind of the medium, to act as counterfeits of Spirit. He told them to leave; their presence aggravated him, and caused confusion because the medium also sensed them.

'This man died on the operating table. I sense his limbs were amputated, but he did not expect to lose them. He was in shock.'

Grace coughed. It was an unconscious response, but Frank could see why her physical body had recalled the energy she had been transferring. She could relate to what she was being told. The cells in her memory centre had been triggered; he saw the ripple of activity in her brain.

Grace nodded. She went to speak but decided against interrupting.

'Stay with me,' he urged. 'Tell me what I need to do.'

The medium was shaking her head slowly. She was concentrating hard, but she was finding it more difficult.

'There's not much more I can see, but this man needs to know who he is. You need to remind him. He is drawn to you because you know him. He will progress when he remembers.'

The woman then directed her thoughts to Frank.

'Grace heard your call for help. She will help you find the light,' she communicated.

'The light?' Frank was confused. It was not light he was seeking.

Frank turned away from Grace and the medium, preferring to find sanctuary with his animal friends.

*

Frank did return to Grace. He felt she was his hope. Despite his confusion at hearing what the medium had said, he knew there was help being offered. He trusted her.

This time, Grace was alone. She was unaware of his presence, but she had prepared for his visit. A candle was lit in the hallway of her home, next to an olive woodcarving of hands in prayer. Beside the ornament, weighted down by a silver crucifix, were newspaper articles and assorted pictures. They had been arranged deliberately to attract attention, but it was the thoughts that had been projected onto these objects that lured Frank's notice.

Instinctively, he knew that they were there for his benefit. As he moved closer, he felt a strong sensation overwhelm him; a feeling of being complete. He felt a connection to every object on the table. He knew that he was looking at images of himself. And those he had known.

The hospital notes showed a scheduled appointment for Mr F Blakely on October 12th 2018, with the ward physiotherapist, Grace Parnell.

Next to the hospital papers was a photocopied newspaper article, dated March 2014, which reported the welcomed safe return of Officer Frank Blakely from 26 Engineer Regiment, who had

incurred serious injuries after his vehicle was sub-
jected to a vehicle-borne suicide attack in Helmand
Province, Afghanistan, in September 2013.

The article included images. Frank recognised
himself as the middle-aged soldier, leaning heavily
on crutches, posing amongst his fellow comrades.
As he studied the photographs of his friends, he
remembered every moment he and his comrades
had shared. He continued to study everything on
the table until he found the source of his emotion.
Lily. The picture of his wife and his son flooded
him with memories and sensations so vivid that his
soul was electrified.

From there, Frank relived every experience he
had known. He recalled the nightmares, the joys,
every moment of his life. Frank remembered every
detail.

He remembered his legs swelling from infection.
The constant pain travelling up his spine, the prolonged physical misery and anguish he had suffered.

He remembered his first meeting with Grace; she
had introduced herself as his physiotherapist who
would begin his treatment following his surgery.
She had kept her promise, having gone to his bedside, but he had not been physically able to fulfil
the appointment. Still, she had sensed him. Her
instinct that there were lingering energies she could
not fathom had induced her to spend time in the
empty ward. Grace was a natural healer; she had
known there was a need for her care, and she had
answered her calling.

He saw all his friends, all his family, all of them around him, helping him. He re-experienced their love and their selflessness towards him. The joy and the thankfulness were bursting forth. Frank remembered why he had held on for so long. As the memory became clear in his mind, Frank felt himself propelled faster than light back to where he had left his heart.

Chapter Fourteen

Winnie

During their married life together, Winnie had enjoyed her times alone with Charles. She preferred his attention to be focused on her, and when there was no-one to judge him, Winnie was satisfied. Her discontent came from seeing how others, people from the upper classes, perceived him. Due to his affable nature, he came across as someone with common habits. He behaved as someone below their class, and therefore he was below hers. But the absence of others meant judgment was exempt and she could relax.

When Charles was not preoccupied with his work in investments, she had enjoyed their days together whilst the children were at boarding school. It had been Charles's insistence that the boys returned home every weekend, and this had been an agreeable compromise. The boys did not feel abandoned, and Winnie had time to focus on herself and her husband without the pressures of motherhood, yet they could still progress as a united family.

That had been many years ago. She had learnt to cope on her own after Charles died, but her life as a widow did not go as she had expected it to. Her harmony with Charles had been conditional. It had depended on privacy, because Winnie could not demonstrate her affection or her acceptance for her husband in public. It was necessary to make it obvious that she did not approve of his jovial nature. For that reason, Winnie did not accompany Charles when he was networking. She was strong and worthy, and it was essential that she was recognised as someone with good breeding and class.

Winnie had expected to be received back into the folds of the elite when Charles had gone. Without him, there was no cause for embarrassment. But she discovered that the aristocracy with whom she had socialised before did not recognise her as being one of their own. Instead, she was publicly humiliated with dismissive scorn. With their privileged education, David and Alexander were friendly with some future dignitaries. The boys had earned their fellowship through years of accompanied study and shared experiences.

She did not have anything to offer. Her beauty had faded, she had no intellectual status, no celebrity background, and therefore no acceptance by the community in which she desired to be included. Her sons had encouraged Winnie to socialise amongst her neighbours, most of whom were middle class and financially comfortable, but Winnie was too obvious a snob. She did not possess Charles's charm, and despite her attempts to integrate herself into the local neighbourhood, she quickly caused offence with her superior attitude.

*

When Winnie was told the cancer treatment had failed, she refused to show fear, because it indicated a lack of control over one's emotions. She had prepared herself to suffer physically as her body succumbed to the disease, and mentally she had taught herself to be strong. The pain medication had helped, and the deep breathing techniques taught by Ellie had provided some benefit, but the lack of distraction from her own inevitable demise had been insufferable.

She had had time to accept it, and now the reality was seen quite simply; she was dying, her life was ending, and the acceptance brought peace and a sense of comfort. Just like one knew they would sleep at the end of the day, she would now sleep at the end of her life. Winnie considered her life now in much the same way. Whereas once she had begun her day with a purpose and reviewed it, she now looked back at her life. Winnie had no regrets.

She had always strived to be the best that she could be. Her life had been conducted with pride and dignity. Winnie had recognised her own worth and demanded that others had valued her, too. Not only had she lived her life fearlessly, she had taken what life had offered. It had offered less than what she had expected, but even though she was without friends in her last days, she saw that friendship could be fickle and short-lived when there lacked the confidence to show the true self. Despite her resolve not to display emotion in public, she now saw that her repressed thoughts of insecurity and envy had been made evident through her acts of resentment or dismissal of others. She had not been as composed as she had thought she was. But Charles had seen her for all that she was. He had seen her cry with joy at the birth of their children and rage with indignation at social rejections. She had laughed with him, she had smiled with him, he had seen her true ways. And not only had he accepted them, but he had loved them. She had done something right.

By opening her heart and allowing Charles to love her, she had allowed him to bring out the best in her.

*

Winnie awoke in the early hours of the morning and knew it was time. The end was here. Her limbs were feeling lighter, as if her body had started to separate into layers. Heat was accumulating towards her upper body. Charles was becoming more persistently obvious. Even David sensed his father was there. He had recognised Charles's scent, although he had dismissed it as his imagination.

Winnie fluttered a hand for attention. She found she was almost too weak to speak, but she could hear David clearly as he spoke gently, instinctively holding his mother's hand towards the warmth of his chest. 'We're here, Mum. It's ok, we are all here.'

Winnie croaked incoherently.

David placed her right hand down on the bed. She felt activity pass to the other side of the bed as her left hand was picked up. She attempted to turn toward where she perceived Alexander to be.

'Yes, I am here, too, Mum.' The slow American drawl was affected.

Charles stepped forward. 'Come on, my girl,' he said. 'We have a party to go to.'

Winnie allowed herself to be pulled out of the bed towards the light that beckoned from the corner of the room. She was beside Charles, who took her arm and placed it in the crook of his own. As she walked towards her eternal life with Charles, she hesitated; she wanted to look back. As she did so, she caught a glimpse of her body lying on the bed. She had perfect peripheral vision. The whole room was viewed in one glance, where David was seated alone by the bed, still holding the hand that had grown cold in his.

Chapter Fifteen

Amelia

The voice, when it came, was not recognisable to Amelia as belonging to one person. Strange as it would seem to her conscious mind, she was having a conversation with a highly intelligent light form. When Amelia had questioned whether she was hearing the voice of God, she saw the light form change into different figures – Jesus, Krishna, Buddha; the forms constantly changed into numerous deities, and archetypal images.

'You see what you wish to believe.'

Amelia had entered a building that looked like her former school. They had ventured along corridors, passing doorways that represented different classrooms, workshops, and laboratories.

They had entered the first classroom, which Amelia recognised was the venue for lessons teaching the principles and the uses of religion. Religion was represented as a stepping-stone, carved in beautiful granite that had been laid before a giant screen. For religion, she understood, was the observance of worship.

The light form had encouraged Amelia to sit before the screen so she could watch a montage of images depicting various religious rites, ceremonies, and the manifestation of religious emotions.

'Human experience is aided by the stability of thought. Belief acts as an anchor which grounds you and prevents you from being distracted from your purpose whilst you are experiencing life.

'Some believe in a God, because there comes with faith an ethos that enables the transcendence of positive thought. Religious teachings are based on the principle of sharing positive energy; to respect life, to be thankful. But it does not matter which God you worship whilst you exist on the material plane. The sharing of love and consideration works as a collective consciousness, even when the methodology of worship differs.

'Those who do not worship a particular God do not lack the ability to live fulfilled and positive lives. They simply do not choose to be educated on how to perform as an effectual human. If there is love in their hearts and the desire to share that love, then they are capable of fulfilling their purpose and evolving spiritually.'

As Amelia considered the simplicity of this teaching, she found herself thinking about rioting, conflicts, and acts of terrorism that had been performed in the name of religion.

The light form had seen her thoughts, and in response she was shown images of children praying, angels casting light, colourful festivals, and scenes of her own family gathering at Christmas.

'Religion can be a beautiful thing. When it is used in the way it has been intended, it acts as a stepping-stone towards true spirituality. But some choose to exploit the use of religion to encourage bigotry.'

This made sense, but Amelia questioned why something that was created to bring enhancement to the human experience, to life itself, could be used in such a negative way. Why was it necessary to have negative influences disrupting everything that could be so good?

They ventured towards another classroom. As they entered, a labyrinth of stairs appeared before them, constantly revolving. They moved slowly, but Amelia was unable to ascend the stairs closer to her. She felt herself being held back whilst the staircase approached closer, then moved away. Amelia noticed that the stairs were varied in style and composition. Some were carved in beautiful wood, others stone, some looked like they were crumbling with age, others showed signs of restoration, some were beautifully clean, whilst others looked neglected and worn.

'Every form of religion – from ancient to modern, high or low, Occidental, Oriental – has their own sub-plane which is accessible for those who wish to continue their faiths and practices. Here, disciples gather, worship, and rejoice.

'There are lower forms of religion, where souls can descend to the lower sub-planes to practise degraded acts of worship. Those who do not believe in the ascension of spirit will be found on the lower sub-plane, convinced they are still on the material plane, for their closed minds have limited their evolvement.'

They turned away from the labyrinth and passed down the corridor to a lecture theatre. The room was occupied, so they did not enter but stood in the doorway as philosophers, metaphysicians, and scientists combined their intelligence, discussing the riddles of reality.

'There will always be opposing thoughts on why life has been created, why existence requires belief systems, for every belief system becomes a religion in its own form. There is no obligation to worship, or to live in a way that is deemed correct or otherwise. That is the gift of free will. Every life form is granted the gift of free will. You can choose what you believe, how to show faith in what you believe, who you love, how you love; there are no rules, because there is no judgement other than the judgement you impose on yourselves. Even when there are principles asserted on you by communities or nations, you have the ability to listen to your own hearts and minds, because ultimately you have an individual purpose. You choose your own road, and by pleasing others or conforming to their ideals you are not following your path, but theirs. That will eventually create an obstacle for you, as it could for them. By being so focused on their attempts to conform to your way of life, they lose their own way.

'That is not to say that you cannot be inspired by others. Often, you will experience other beliefs or practices that will attract or repel you, and this is how you are reminded which path you are meant to follow.'

They passed many classrooms, some of which were sealed closed, forbidding entry.

'There are some realms where only the most evolved souls with the highest spiritual under-standing and truest heart will be allowed to venture. Visitors are forbidden entry. It is strictly guarded, for they are sacred places.'

The workshop was situated at the end of the corridor.

'This is where astral templates are created and invented. They are designs for many great works that are achieved on the material plane. Every musical composition, every technological invention, every great piece of literature or artwork, is a reproduction that has been rendered using these templates.'

Next, Amelia was shown the laboratory. They did not enter the room, but were able to watch intense activity happening within by viewing through a window.

'No energy is wasted. Everything is recycled. All life has the power to redeem and heal itself, so there will always be the reconfiguring of ideas and discarding the new modes of thought to make way for new impressions. There is always advancement, so here is where old mental material is dissected and analysed, with the purpose of finding methods of progress.'

They left the building and exited large doors that opened into an expanse of green grass. It stretched miles ahead.

'Space without distractions enables freedom to express all aspirations and emotions.'

They were now outside the school. The light form encircled her, and she felt everything that she had been taught being absorbed deep into her memory.

'What you have been shown is a condensed view of how free will enables you to pick and choose what feels right for you. After you return to your life, it is inevitable that you will come across prejudice and other forms of negative feedback from those who wish you to conform to their ideologies. Human existence requires some control, and there are those that have the purpose of asserting a level of control in order to ensure survival of the human race. So, there are many conflicting episodes one will encounter throughout their lives.

'A parent will control their child's movements with the belief that they are keeping their child safe; an educator will demand certain behaviour of their students to ensure their teachings are applied; just like a nation will have laws to protect their communities. However, eventually the child, the student, or the citizen, will develop their own preferences, and will follow their own instinct by using the free will they have been granted. This is how children became adults, students become workers, and citizens become agents.'

Amelia nodded. 'So, how am I to use what I have just learnt?'

The light form encircled her with warmth as it pushed her forward and upwards.

'You are now ready to see how this intelligence can be employed.'

Chapter Sixteen

Frank

Daniel had fallen asleep with his hands still holding the iPad that Frank had bought him on his twelfth birthday, much to Lily's disapproval. 'You've given him the opportunity to disengage from us entirely!' she had admonished. But even she had recognised that her son was getting older, and spending all his free time with his parents wasn't as much fun for him as it used to be.

Frank gazed around his son's bedroom. There were family photographs pinned on a cork board, memorabilia from family days out at theme parks or holidays, Daniel's childish drawings; the assorted images spoke volumes of the happy life they had all shared together.

Every moment since Daniel's birth, Frank had appreciated how blessed he was. His love for his son was immeasurable. He had kissed Daniel's head and cheeks thousands of times, but it had never felt he had done so enough. He had embraced his son with heartfelt sincerity, yet his arms had felt they could squeeze harder to lock the love into his son's psyche. It was impossible to express the depth of his devotion towards Daniel.

Frank gazed at the sleeping boy with wonder and pride. He could see the future that was laid before him and knew his boy would do well in life. Daniel was sensitive and young, and from his new vantage point, Frank could read that his energies were bright and receptive, not dulled or weighted down through grief. It gave Frank an opening through which to communicate.

Frank entered his child's dream. He invited him to a game of football, something he had known Daniel had always wanted to do but that Frank's physical condition had denied. Now, with the aid of imagination, they played with endless energy, running across the field together, congratulating one another for their skills, their mutual joy expressed through high five hand-slaps and playful punching. After they had fallen on the ground panting with exhaustion, he walked his son to a bench and sat him down.

'I've come to say goodbye, son.'

Daniel nodded; he understood. 'I thought you were coming home,' he said.

'So did I, son.' Frank encircled his arm around Daniel. It felt real and solid. Daniel leaned against his father; he was a child again, needing his father to hold him and comfort him.

'I need you to be brave for your mum,' Frank said.

'I have, Dad. I have been brave. I don't let her see me cry.'

Frank kissed his son's head. 'No, that is not what I meant. It's ok to cry. Crying is good. It's how you will heal. Your mum needs to see you cry, that way she will understand how you are coping.

'Don't block her out, Daniel. Let her in, tell her how you feel, share your grief with her. You are going to get angry, but that is ok. Don't be ashamed that you are angry with me. I understand. You feel I left you, but I haven't, son, and I never will. I forgot where I was for a bit, but now I am here, and I will be here again.

'You have a long, wonderful future ahead of you, and I am going to make sure that I share all the events with you. I will! Just remember that life is a journey; it's going to be confusing, sometimes difficult, but fill it with love and laughter as much as you can. And I promise you, son, I will laugh and I will cry or shout with you. I will sing with you, dance with you; I will laugh at all your jokes, even though you've never been very good at telling them.

'I promise I will be there with you and your mother.'

Daniel listened. He held his father's hand. 'Can I get a dog?' he asked.

Frank laughed. 'Sure! I will do what I can. I don't know how, but one thing I do know: miracles happen. You and your mum were miracles in my life. So, yes, you can have a dog. And every time you are with your dog, know that I sent it to you to look after you in ways I can't.

'I will love you forever," Frank said. He kissed Daniel gently, and sent him back to his slumber.

Lily was asleep. She was lying on her stomach with one arm raised up and resting on the pillow above her head. Her face was turned towards the middle of the bed, partially hidden by the duvet that had been pulled up over her chin. The space next to her on the double bed was vacant and undisturbed.

Frank stayed beside the bed watching her, feeling more alive than he had for so long. He wanted to touch her, and reached towards her before hesitating, fearing he would pass through her and shatter the illusion he was granting himself, that he was a physical embodiment of her husband again whilst he said goodbye.

He hovered beside the bed, then attempted to speak her name. There was no sound uttered, but he refused to allow his lack of physicality to deny him this opportunity.

'When we are together, we are one.' Lily's words resurfaced in his memory.

He focused on the words, remembering the depth of her sentiment. She had meant it. The two of them had believed so strongly in their union that nothing was able to separate them or diffuse the love they had shared. Frank focused on this. He imagined the force of their attraction was the strongest link he could manifest in imagination, and then he reached for her. He touched her arm and felt her, truly felt her physical form, and revelled in the smoothness of her skin. She reacted. Her arm moved as if it were being tickled.

'It's me, Lily.'

Frank re-enacted how he had spoken to Grace. But Lily's psyche was injured from grief and it blocked his entry to her dreams, though he tried.

He allowed all the emotion he had stored in his heart to be projected as a powerful force, and imagined himself moving onto the bed, delighting as he found that the mattress sank as he did so. He moved closer to her so that now his face was before hers. He felt her breath on his cheek. The sensation was glorious.

'Lily, I love you. I never meant to leave you without saying goodbye. I'm so sorry, my girl. I thought we would grow old together. I didn't mean to leave you alone, but I will be here when you need me. I promise.

'I remember the time I asked you out. Do you? Do you remember how shy we were? How we kept giggling and interrupting one another, even though we didn't know what to talk about? Do you remember the first time we said, 'I love you'? You said it first, although you deny it, but the truth is I loved you even before then. I've always loved you, Lily. We didn't have the best of times sometimes, I know. I wasn't always easy to live with, but I don't regret a second that I was with you.

'I want you to be happy now, Lily. You need to follow where your heart takes you, with my blessing. If you get the opportunity to love again, do so with an open heart. Do that for Daniel. Do that for our son. I will live on in you both. You will always be my girl, Always and forever. I will be there when it your time, and we will be together again. I promise.

'Be brave, my girl. Know that I love you truly.'

Lily shifted in her sleep and rolled onto her back. Her eyes partially opened but she remained unconscious. 'Frank?' she murmured. A tear slipped down her cheek and over her nose. 'I miss you.'

'I know, but it's ok. Everything is ok. Goodbye, my love.'

Frank felt himself drifting; he couldn't maintain the physical form he had created for this moment. He kissed her on the forehead and turned away for the last time.

Chapter Seventeen

Winnie

David had spent two hours arranging the bouquets, and now he allowed himself some time to admire the various displays. Every flower had been chosen with care, not only for their fragrance but for their meaning. David did not expect his mother to be able to see his accomplishment, but he hoped somehow that the love he was expressing in the floral displays would find its way to her.

When the coffin arrived, they would enter the foyer, breathing in the heady scent of blue hyacinths that had been planted in small wicker baskets and placed on window ledges and small tables, next to the order of service booklets. It had been a challenge to find some late bloomers in March, but the few David had found were enough to convey a message of sincerity.

He swallowed the lump from his throat and fussed over the vase he had placed on a small table near the entrance of the Chapel. Sprigs of rosemary had been included in the bouquet, not just to create a calm atmosphere, but also to honour the occasion of remembrance; the freesia highlighted the high spirits and thoughtfulness behind each arrangement; and the deep purple lavender, the colour of royalty, honoured Winnie in the way she would expect, representing the elegance and refinement she had always strived for. Posies of jasmine, gardenia and pink roses had been bound with lilac ribbon and tied to the end of each pew.

David was aware that there would be no guests to share the message. And even if there were unexpected visitors attending to pay their last respects, they would be fooled into thinking they were attending a wedding rather than a funeral. However, this was not an issue of contention. In David's mind, the joy of a wedding could be applied to his mother's funeral. Her passing was not just an occasion for his own mourning, but of gratitude for the life she had experienced and shared. Knowing that she was no longer in discomfort or suffering the indignity of her latter fragility, was a cause for happiness. At the front of the church, where his mother would be laid for the last prayers, a large display of lisianthus waited for her.

He had arranged for similar bouquets to travel with his mother in the hearse. Winnie may never know the message David had been so keen to express, but the lisianthus had been his chosen expression of gratitude for the life he had shared with her, the devotion he had offered, and the blessing of her ever-lasting bond with Charles, with whom she would no doubt be resting in eternal peace.

David had not admitted that the regular delivery of flowers to her bedside had been his gift to her. He had needed her to believe that Alexander had not abandoned his mother, and he had been reassured by the comfort that his deception had given her. In her last days, Winnie had become more confused and withdrawn. It was a natural progression, and he had been warned by the medical professionals that Winnie would behave in an irrational manner. So, whilst her dismissal of him had been hurtful, he had not expected his mother to have been appreciative.

He checked his watch; the hearse was due to arrive soon. David cast a critical eye over the decorations, tweaked a few strands here and there, and walked home before the hearse arrived.

*

The funeral procession was short. Other than the funeral director walking in front of the hearse and the pallbearers inside the vehicle, the only other attendees were Winnie's nurse, Ellie, and David. Alexander had declined to come; he used his busy work schedule and the long journey from California as an excuse, but David understood. It was easier to maintain distance rather than confront the reality that their mother had gone.

It had been considered that the lack of mourners would justify a less traditional approach, but David had believed Winnie would have wanted to have a public display of respect. So, he had insisted that the funeral cortège begin at the house, and they walk the three-quarters of a mile to the church.

Ellie had grumbled on account of her corns, although she had complied. It was not the worst chore she had had to do for Winnie, and secretly she felt sympathy toward David, who yet again had been left to manage on his own. He was a good man; sensitive and considerate. She had seen him go to the trouble of pretending to be his brother for the last few weeks, which she knew had not been easy.

At first, hearing David practise an American accent had been rather amusing, but when she saw how much effort he had put into his disguise, her heart ached for him. His brother hadn't deserved to be let off so easy. She would have liked to tell Alexander a few home truths over the phone, but she had resisted the temptation. It was none of her business any more. Winnie had not been an easy patient, with her high and mighty airs, but she had been a decent human being, and David was a man who needed some support. As far as Ellie was concerned, this was an act of closure.

David had insisted on joining the pallbearers carry his mother into the chapel. As they set the coffin down gently, David rested a single daffodil bidding farewell and two pink carnations on top of the coffin. As he did so, the emotion welled over him.

As a child, his father had told David that pink carnations had germinated from the Virgin Mary's tears shed over Jesus's death, and ever since had been the symbol of a mother's undying love. David did not doubt his mother had loved her sons – the love had not always been equally shared, but David appreciated Winnie for the love and security she had offered. Alexander had not sent any flowers, but he had asked David to choose a floral donation on his behalf. So whilst David's last offering had been small and simple, the meaning had been the most poignant.

Ellie and David listened to the short précis of Winnie's life, prayed in gratitude for the life she had lived, and sang *Amazing Grace*, which David had requested knowing that Winnie would have appreciated the irony. Then David read a short passage he had chosen from Ecclesiastes. Winnie had not been one to read the Bible, but David knew she had attended church as a child with her mother, so he had chosen a passage that he felt was appropriate to his mother's understanding in life.

There is a time for everything, and a season for every activity under the heavens: a time to be born and a time to die, a time to plant and a time to uproot, a time to kill and a time to heal, a time to tear down and a time to build, a time to weep and a time to laugh, a time to mourn and a time to dance...

*

David stayed long after Ellie and the celebrant had left. He sat in the church garden and allowed the emotion to be released. For the last five months, he had tried to act as strong as he could, witnessing his mother's deterioration with a clinical attitude. Whilst he was with her, he had remained positive, efficient, and patient, but every time he had left her bedside, he had experienced rage. He was so angry at the cruelty of the disease that had ravaged her intelligence, reducing her to a disorientated, irrational sufferer. Once so noble, she had been forced to suffer the indignity of soiling herself and to be reliant on a stranger washing her.

There had been moments when David had left the house and driven to a remote area where he would scream at the heavens, pleading with God to show her mercy. He had shouted, punched the car seat beside him until his rage subsided, and then returned to his mother's bedside. If there had been a way of taking the pain from her, he would have done so at any cost.

But looking back, David had no regrets. He had done the very best he could. Winnie had died knowing she was loved, and that she had not been alone.

The tears cascaded down his face. He gave up trying to wipe them away and allowed the emotion to flow unchecked. He sobbed until he was exhausted.

David sat for a long while. He imagined Winnie being with his father, and the thought comforted him. He retrieved his mobile from his jacket pocket, deciding it was time to email Alexander and share details of the service with him.

Alexander needed to know that the service had honoured Winnie in the way she would have expected. David's brother had adopted an air of cool aloofness, but in reality, Alexander could be sensitive and emotional. Their mother had never known that Alexander had found love, that he had been married for over ten years. Although she would have been reassured Alexander was happy, she would not have approved of her son being in love with another man. She would have wanted Alexander to have the freedom to have been admired by many, without being weighed down in a committed relationship.

In comparison, Winnie had wanted David to get married. She had asserted her belief that it would bring out the man in him. Yet when David did get married, she had disapproved strongly of her daughter-in-law. A headstrong, vain woman, she had made it clear she did not want children, but then had left David within two years of their marriage, pregnant by another man. She had failed to see the irony that David had fallen in love with a woman who had repeated his mother's example.

David composed the message to his younger brother with consideration, knowing that he was experiencing heartbreak at the passing of their mother, but coping as best he could by maintaining distance. Alexander would not have coped seeing their mother so ill.

After the message was sent, David continued to sit whilst he contemplated what he would do next.

He had resigned from his employment in marketing and sold his apartment so that he could care for Winnie full-time. Alexander would be the sole recipient of his mother's estate as she had requested, but David had enough to buy a place of his own. Now it was his opportunity to live the life that would make him happy. He looked down at the broken stem of a freesia flower that he had retrieved from the chapel floor and considered it for some time. Persevere, it said to him.

Then he stood up, smoothed down his trousers, and wandered over to the wall of remembrance where he searched for his father's name. He found the brass plaque, recently polished, on the middle row nearest the rose garden. He stood there for a second, kissed the freesia, and slotted the stem gently between the wall and the back of the plaque.

As David walked back to the house, he considered he had several weeks to tidy his mother's affairs, and then he would begin a new life. The sun was shining. Spring was on its way.

Chapter Eighteen

Amelia

Amelia was soaring; the flight was effortless and incredible. She was weightless, being carried by her own euphoria. Everything she looked upon filled her with joy and awe.

There was light everywhere, colours of every hue shimmering and energising. She passed through a veil and experienced life from the beginning, as the first of mankind, then looked to the side and saw the present and the future of mankind stretched hundreds of years ahead. Every life experience was happening in one moment.

She saw astral dwellers engaged in their recreation. As they contributed to earthly intellectual ambitions and aspirations, they worked earnestly and joyfully.

She flew higher and faster until the earth was a tiny speck behind her.

Around her, the solar system whizzed past with speed and light. She ventured further into the galaxy, every moment absorbing knowledge and understanding, her mental capacity limitless.

Thousands of different worlds that she looked upon were magnificent and varied. Billions of life forms passed by her, every dimension bursting with life and creation. Amelia could see everything, even though she was passing at incredible speed.

Amelia flew further and further, noting every differentiation in the atmospheres. She could taste, hear, see, and feel indescribable sensations, experiencing every creation in the Universe.

As she ventured forward still, the light became brighter. Passing into this new light, she found she was in the beginning of time, where all creation had begun. The light embraced her, absorbed her, and she at one with all consciousness, the divine source of all creation. Amelia was vacuumed further into the centre of the light, and there she understood the absolute truth. There is no death, there is no end. Life is immortal.

*

The windchimes tinkled gently. Amelia found herself alone on her grandparents' sofa. She was exultant by her journey, but knew instinctively it was time to return to her physical form and resume her purpose, which was now very clear to her. The voice that she heard in her mind was gentle but firm.

'You have been shown the simplest of all truths; that all life belongs to one collective consciousness. There are no limitations to what you can achieve, other than what you imagine to be obstacles. You recognise that there is greater meaning to every experience; there is no event more important than another. Even the most trivial details can be the most relevant. No person is less important than another, just like one life is not more or less worthy than another. There is no hierarchy, no priority, no bias, and no judgement. Every creation is a miracle because it all comes from one divine source. Life is a gift that is to be shared.'

Amelia could see glimpses of the life she would return to. There would be moments of great happiness, and times that were to give her many challenges. The scenes flashed before her, one after another, as she was reminded of her life's plan. There was no hesitation in her wanting to resume her life, despite what she saw.

'With this understanding, you can recognise all the potentials that are laid before you. Be thankful for the opportunities and for what have been achieved thus far. Be fearless and allow others to see who you truly are. Love the person you are. Allow yourself to love others as your equals, by sharing all that you are, your understanding and your experiences. And inspire others with your faith.'

Amelia was lifted by two enormous life forms. She glanced back and saw her grandparents smiling and becoming smaller, until they faded into the distance as she was carried away.

The suddenness of being thrown was forceful, almost violent. Amelia was jolted back into her life.

Chapter Nineteen

Frank

Frank found Grace in her armchair, knitting baby clothes. She was content sharing her gifts for the benefit of others. The knitting was like a meditation for her; her mind was relaxed, her body comfortable in the chair, but still she breathed with effort. Her heart was working hard. It was struggling. She had helped him in ways she would likely never know. Grace had been his guardian angel, which was, he realised, the most ironic of all, considering that all this time it had been him that had been dead. But she had guided and rescued him, and his heart sent her his appreciation and the promise he would repay her kindness.

Grace was not aware of Frank. It was as if she had become numb to his energy, but he preferred it that way. It would make it easier to say goodbye.

He had returned to Grace with a purpose. For so long he had been imprisoned by his fear, but Grace had set him free. His freedom had brought him understanding, and he realised now that what he had once considered great mysteries in life were nothing of the kind. He had lived practising the simple truth, and yet had not been aware that the heart was the wisest part of the human soul. He had loved deeply when he was alive, but he had fooled himself to believe that his broken body had also broken his heart.

Grace had shown him otherwise. Frank moved closer to her and willed the vibrations to slow down, then he imagined he was resting his hand directly on her heart.

He applied all that he had learnt; that everything was composed of light, and every soul a conduit of energy. It was instinctive how he allowed light to channel through him into Grace. He stayed there thanking her, thanking the Universe for sending her to him, and he saw what it was that had ailed her.

'Your heart is heavy from sadness, Grace, and it is suffering. Release the burden that you carry. You may not have given birth to children of your own, but you have nurtured me, and you will nurture many more. You have shown so much love and you have brought so much happiness. Now it's your time to discover joy. Let yourself laugh, Grace. The more laughter you have, the less illness. Be healed.'

Frank stepped away. He could still feel the energy flooding through him, and he turned his focus to where it came from. The light was above him, raining down like a shower of energy. He allowed himself to rise towards it, and immediately felt himself being lifted. His ascent had begun.

Chapter Twenty

Amelia

Amelia did not expect her recuperation to be simple, but she had not expected it to be so difficult either. Learning to deal with the pain was not easy, but the greater difficulty was interacting when her mind was so dazed. It was not the pain medication that caused her mental unease, although that did make her drowsy. She felt as if she had been away in a foreign land for so long that now she did not know how to communicate in her native language. Amelia remembered most of her out-of-body experience. It returned in disjointed fragments of memory, but now she was back in a physical realm, it was difficult to accept it had been real. It had not been a dream, she knew that, for she had an intelligence she had not possessed before, and emotions she had not previously experienced. But to allow herself to remember her spiritual experience seemed inappropriate to her current situation.

Amelia had been in a coma for six days, but her parents looked as if they had aged a few years with worry. Amelia responded to them with compassion and gratitude. She had apologised to her family for the anguish she had caused them, and she had thanked them for their love and their healing. Her mother had cried as Amelia expressed her gratitude; her father had bent over her, embracing her as best he could without causing her more pain.

Amelia knew she was paralysed from the waist down. She knew before the doctor had told her, but she also knew there was hope. It was difficult to gauge how the spine would recover, but there was a possibility of a full recovery. It might be within the next year, or maybe longer... if at all. It was frightening, but Amelia knew she would cope.

She told her parents the same. They had wept and nodded, agreeing that they would all work together as a team. Michael had smiled and cheekily asked if he could use her bedroom if she was being moved downstairs. He had meant it with light humour, but she had agreed anyway.

The stay in hospital lasted twelve weeks, and was spent coming to terms with her new condition. There would inevitably be a period of adjustment, but as the weeks passed, Amelia found she could occupy herself without the need for her family's constant presence. Her parents had returned to work but with reduced hours, and Michael was at school again during the week.

It was quite deliberate that Amelia chose a time when her family was not around before she allowed herself to look at her reflection. She had been warned that she had incurred deep facial lacerations, and she had fingered the stitches across her right brow and cheek. But it had taken a moment of courage before she could actually look at them. It was a shock. She had screamed when she saw her features had become a patchwork of repaired flesh, but just the once. Then she had passed the mirror back to the nurse, thanked her for the reassurance that the stitches would fade in time, and sank into a medicated fog.

*

The physiotherapist visited Amelia two days before her discharge from hospital.

'I will see you twice a week to begin with. Together, we will practise pain management whilst improving your circulation, reduce muscle atrophy, and work to improve your overall health and wellness.' Grace spoke reassuringly to her new patient after she had introduced herself. She spoke with the melodic hint of a lady of West Indian descent; her eyes were bright and wide with sincerity, giving her a trustworthy demeanour, as she sat on the chair beside Amelia, her hands, bedecked with numerous rings on her fingers, clasped in her lap.

'It won't be easy,' she said. 'Part of the treatment is learning to retrain your brain as well as your body to regain some or possibly all of your lost mobility.'

Amelia bit her lip anxiously as she contemplated the struggle ahead of her, but Grace smiled with understanding and patted her hand gently.

'It's ok,' she said. 'You are facing a challenge, but we will get through it together. There is no rush. Take every day at a time. First, adjust to being back at home, and I will see you soon.'

Grace beamed at her and bent down over Amelia before she left. She waggled a heavily ringed finger in front of Amelia's face with mock authority.

'Believe me, young lady, there is always hope. You hold onto that and only good can happen.' Grace offered a gentle squeeze to the back of Amelia's hand and beamed with sincerity before leaving Amelia to think of home.

*

The sound of Michael strumming on the guitar could be heard from the room above her. He had been playing a short while, and Amelia imagined him sitting on the edge of his bed with his guitar resting loosely on his lap, his head tilted slightly to one side as he improvised, feeling the vibrations reverberate through the body of the instrument. Amelia used to find his habit annoying. Any noise Michael produced was previously a cause for irritation, but on this occasion, she appreciated the melody.

'It sounds good!' she called up to the room above.

The strumming paused momentarily. 'Thanks,' Michael called back.

Amelia smiled. Her brother was rather special, after all.

*

Amelia had practised her stretching exercises with a determined focus, but now she was exhausted. She had had enough for one day. For the last eight sessions, Grace had insisted that Amelia remained in a standing position for as long as she could. It was a shock, considering that Amelia had no feelings in her lower limbs, but Grace had been relentless.

'I thought you were nice.' Amelia spoke through gritted teeth. She was sweaty, her face was itchy and hot.

Grace laughed gently. 'I am, dear. If I don't make you do this, you are likely to suffer more than just a prolonged lack of mobility. The muscle spasms are bad enough, but you don't want to add to your troubles by getting a bowel or an urinary tract infection!'

Amelia continued forward, both arms taking the weight of her body by holding the side bars, as she dragged her legs behind her.

She had made progress. Her upper body strength had improved considerably since her physiotherapy treatment had begun, but she needed a rest and Grace was not easily manipulated. Amelia had cried, cursed, and shouted at Grace, but the older woman did not succumb to the attempted emotional blackmail. Her focus was on Amelia's recovery, and despite the agony that she was forcing her patient to endure, it was obvious that the girl's recovery was just as important to Grace.

Eventually, the gruelling session had expired. Amelia lay on her back as Grace manipulated the joints.

'So, have you considered what you are going to do with all your free time?' Grace questioned. She had removed her rings whilst she was working with Amelia, and had stored them in a small plastic wallet which had been placed on the table nearby.

Amelia studied them; there must be over twelve rings, she calculated, all worn at the same time.

'I'm undecided. I may go back to college in September and redo the last year, but I don't know that my heart is in it any more.'

'So you will find something else maybe.'

Amelia sighed, unconvinced. She lacked inspiration.

Grace lifted Amelia's left leg and pulled it gently. 'Well, you need to do something! Do you have a nice young man who will take you out?'

Amelia shook her head, unconscious of the long sigh she emitted as she thought of Ollie.

'Aha!' Grace laughed and returned Amelia's leg to the table. She left the room and returned, wiping her hands on a towel that she then discarded in the laundry bin. She retrieved her rings and slid them back onto her fingers as she sat down on the chair next to the physio table.

'Whoever he is, he is a very lucky man to get your attention.' Grace winked.

Amelia smiled, appreciating Grace's kind words. 'I don't think he will be interested in me.'

'How will you know if you don't try?' Grace leaned forward. 'My girl, let me tell you. You've got to believe!' Hints of the Caribbean accent became stronger as her enthusiasm for the subject heightened. 'A year ago, I would have expected to have been either dead or retired. My heart was struggling; I was sick!'

With a sudden movement from her chair, Grace stood up and opened her arms out wide. 'Now I dance! You see me shimmering and shaking my black booty like a Jamaican carnival queen!' She laughed as she saw Amelia's dubious expression, then danced around Amelia with her head thrown back, her large teeth on full display.

'Yes, it's true! Now I dance and I laugh as much as I can. My heart is as strong as an ox. It's a miracle, my girl. So, you have to believe, too! Believe in yourself!'

Grace ceased her merry dance around the table and eased Amelia back into her wheelchair. 'So, do you believe?' She bent down and stared at Amelia directly, in an almost confrontational manner.

Amelia smiled. 'Actually...' she said, 'I do. I really do.'

The flower shop looked beautiful, but it was the fragrance of the flowers that beckoned Amelia closer. An extensive palette of colours had been arranged so that the taller blooms graduated down to the shorter stems, in lined wicker baskets. Chandeliers hung from the centre of the gallery. The twinkling lights reflected in the mirror hung above the counter, and gave the impression of vastness.

The man smiled a welcome as Amelia wheeled herself towards the open doorway. 'I apologise for any disarray,' he said. 'I'm not officially open yet, but you are welcome to come in and browse.'

Amelia accepted his invitation and wheeled herself further into the shop. 'It looks so beautiful,' she said. 'The scent is incredible!'

The man laughed in agreement, then came forward to shake her hand. 'I'm David,' he said. He followed her gaze and selected a flower that she had been studying and handed it to her.

'What is this flower?' Amelia looked closely at the exotic bloom she cradled in her hand. It reminded her of similar blooms she had seen during her out-of-body experience. In her mind she saw a fantastic design for a bag made of vivid crushed velvets, in rich greens, oranges, and mauves. This flower was the inspiration she had hoped for.

'It's a strelitzia, but sometimes it is called the crane flower or the Bird of Paradise. It is native to South Africa. It is rather wonderful, isn't it? It is often given as a gesture of faithfulness. Keep it.' David declined to accept the flower back. 'Consider it as your own piece of paradise on earth."

David bustled around the shop, explaining that he was due to open the following morning. He was excited, and his enthusiasm was infectious. Amelia found herself venturing further and examining the floral displays.

'I don't suppose you would be interested in hiring me as an assistant?' she found herself asking.

David smiled. 'I would love to, but I'm afraid it's impossible to afford any staff at this time. I cannot guarantee how successful I will be yet. But I do know they are looking to hire at the bistro down the road.'

Amelia's eyebrows shot up. 'They are?'

David straightened his back, resting his hands on his hips, and looked down the road towards the small coffee shop Amelia had once frequented.

'An old schoolfriend of mine owns it, but she has handed the reins over to her son, my godson Oliver, or Ollie as he prefers to be called. Why don't you go there now and have a chat with him? I'm sure he can offer you some work. It's worth a try. Tell him David recommended you.'

*

The nervous energy was coursing through Amelia. She felt jittery and excited as she wheeled herself down the road towards the bistro. But as she got closer, a dark bundle of energy no taller than eight inches tall came bounding towards her, dragging a young boy behind him. Amelia instinctively retrieved the flower she had kept on her lap and held it away from the small dog that was now so excited to introduce itself it was trying to jump onto her lap. The boy gently picked the dog up in his arms.

'Wobble! Naughty! No more!" He tapped the dog's nose with a gentle forefinger before placing the animal back on the ground as he addressed Amelia. 'I am so sorry. He gets so excited. I'm trying to train him, but it's going to take a while."

Amelia smiled and admired the dog; it looked at her with large brown eyes and an inviting expression.

'Did I hear you call him Wobble? That's a great name!' She smiled at the dog and blew it kisses, which it clearly understood to be an invitation for a cuddle and attempted to jump onto her lap again. She did not resist, and reassured the boy that she welcomed the affection. As soon as the dog jumped up, it nuzzled her and sniffed her neck. The sensation made Amelia giggle. Sensing encouragement, the dog continued to lavish love on his new friend.

'A neighbour of ours breeds Havanese dogs, but she couldn't sell Wobble because he has one leg shorter than the others, so he walks funny. He was going to be put in a rescue home, but Mum said we could have him.'

Amelia smiled. 'He really is gorgeous. You're very lucky to have such a lovely friend.' She gently encouraged Wobble off her lap as the boy smiled at his dog with pride.

'I know,' he said. 'He's my best friend for life.'

The dog gave an impatient yap and they ran off, followed seconds later by a young woman rushing towards them. Her handbag slapped against her thigh. Strands of ash blonde hair had worked loose from her hairband and suckered themselves onto her face with the perspiration. Her face was flushed as she paused by Amelia who was still stationary, allowing passage past the wheelchair on the narrow pavement.

'I'm so sorry!' the woman gasped, holding her hand on her chest as she struggled to catch her breath. 'I hope they didn't bother you?'

Amelia reassured her, and the woman continued on her pursuit, calling as she ran, 'Daniel, don't encourage him to run by the road! Make him sit at the kerb!'

The smell of cinnamon and coffee was intoxicating, even outside the coffee shop. In her moment of courage, she wheeled herself forward too quickly and knocked the leg of one of the outside tables with the wheel of her chair. The menu fell off and landed beyond her reach. She struggled to lean forward but was stopped in her attempts.

'It's ok, I've got it.'

Amelia's breath caught in her throat as she looked up at the young man she had admired for so long. Ollie was apologetic as he moved the table and chairs further away from her, enabling a wider entry.

'I am so sorry. I normally place these wider apart. We often get lots of prams with shopping bags hanging off the handlebars, so we always get knocked furniture. I should know better.'

He invited her into the shop and returned to the back of the counter. 'What can I get you?'

Amelia ordered a hazelnut latte. She waited as he occupied himself and then her voice seemed to boom out much louder than she had intended. "I don't know if you remember me, but I used to come here quite often.'

Ollie turned to face her. 'Yes, I remember,' he said. 'Welcome back! Millie, isn't it?'

'Amelia,' she corrected him, but felt a surge of delight. He remembered her! 'David suggested I come here. He said you were looking to hire someone.'

'Crikey! Good for David! Yes, I am, but I haven't got around publishing a vacancy yet! Why? Are you interested?'

Amelia nodded, and then hesitated. 'Of course, it may be tricky with my chair...' Her voice trailed off, suddenly becoming self-conscious. Who was she kidding? She had already knocked a table just trying to enter the establishment!

Ollie crafted a silhouette of a girl's profile in the milk froth and displayed it with an almost shy grin. 'It doesn't do you justice. I'm still practising.' He offered to take it over to the table nearest the wall and she accepted his invitation, but was surprised when Ollie sat down on the chair next to her.

'I don't think your chair will be a problem,' he said. 'You can serve customers just as easily, and I may need help with sandwich deliveries at lunchtimes. We used to use the services of an online food ordering and delivery service, but to be honest, it cut into our profits more than we wanted. Most of our customers are in offices with lifts, so that wouldn't be much of an issue either. I'd be happy to try you, if you are really interested?'

Amelia nodded, possibly a little too enthusiastically.

'You look well, considering what you have been through.' Ollie changed the subject so quickly that Amelia blushed, realising the attention was now on her.

Instinctively, her hand rose to her scar. 'I'm not looking so good actually, but this will fade, eventually. I may even walk again, too.'

Ollie leaned forward and studied the scar quite intently. 'It's actually rather beautiful,' he said. They both laughed. 'No, seriously. The mark on your cheek looks like a butterfly; it would be a shame if it fades too much.'

Amelia found herself almost mute with delight.

He stood up suddenly. 'Sorry, I've got to get back to work, but enjoy your coffee. Consider it a perk of the job. All staff get free refreshments!' He leaned over and shook her hand firmly. 'Give me a few days to get the paperwork sorted, and I'll see you Monday. We open at seven. Is that ok?'" He waited until she nodded, then smiled and returned to the counter.

'Thank you, thank you, thank you!' Amelia whispered to the heavens. She imagined her prayer rocketing into the Universe as a huge ball of white light. Maybe it was her imagination... but she was sure she heard the tinkling of windchimes.